YOU ARE LOVED

NOVELLAS

ANDREW MALAN MILWARD

YOU ARE LOVED

NOVELLAS

ANDREW MALAN MILWARD

SOUTHEAST MISSOURI STATE UNIVERSITY PRESS | 2024

ISBN: 979-8-9868593-4-7
Softcover: $19.95

First published in 2024 by
Southeast Missouri State University Press
One University Plaza, MS 2650
Cape Girardeau, MO 63701
www.semopress.com

Cover by Elina Cohen

Library of Congress Cataloging-in-Publication Data

Names: Milward, Andrew Malan, author.
Title: You are loved : novellas / Andrew Malan Milward.
Identifiers: LCCN 2023052925 | ISBN 9798986859347 (paperback)
Subjects: LCGFT: Novellas.
Classification: LCC PS3613.I59199 Y68 2024 | DDC 813/.6--dc23/eng/20231127
LC record available at https://lccn.loc.gov/2023052925

For Buster

CONTENTS

"It is said that the camera cannot lie, but rarely do we allow it to do anything else, since the camera sees what you point it at: the camera sees what you want it to see. The language of the camera is the language of our dreams."
—James Baldwin, *The Devil Finds Work*

"Photography is an elegiac art, a twilight art. Most subjects photographed are, by virtue of being photographed, touched with pathos….All photographs are memento mori."
—Susan Sontag, *On Photography*

"Why is the measure of love loss?"
—Jeanette Winterson, *Written on the Body*

My Passion, My Becoming

When you're born and come of age in Mississippi, as I was, and it feels like your long-term survival depends on escape, as I did, there are only two pathways from which one might make that jump to the wider world: Memphis or New Orleans. For me the choice was easy enough. After graduating college in the spring of 1998, I moved to New Orleans, where I lived in an apartment in the Marigny that belonged to my stepmother, who spent most of the year in Houston, and who generously allowed me to live there rent-free because I was saving money for graduate school. For two years I worked in a small law office, where I did secretarial work—filing, sorting, typing letters and memos, changing the coffee filters—that earned me ten dollars an hour. I spent my days in the office, sometimes quite busy with tasks, while other times I had long stretches with nothing to do, so I'd taken to photocopying the chapters of whatever book I was reading and slipping them into clients' folders so that I could read on the job. If one of the law partners or paralegals came by my desk while I was reading, I would squint hard at the pages, as if really engrossed in my work when I was really lost in whatever dream the writer was creating for me. I read the better part of *Ulysses* that way.

In the evenings after work, I'd go home and study for the GRE or fuss over photographs I'd taken that I hoped would gain me admission to a strong fine arts program, but often they left me unsatisfied, so I'd wander out into the night with my camera, to the madness of the Quarter or to the music of Frenchman Street, imagining myself a stealthy street photographer like Vivian Maier or Garry Winogrand. Some nights I took long walks through the Bywater to the Industrial Canal or uptown to the Garden District or Irish Chanel, sometimes into Treme and Bayou St. John. People warned me about the danger, the city's propensity for violence, which was just as strong as its propensity for revelry and good cheer, but no one ever bothered me on my walks around the city, when I—before I even knew the word—fancied myself something of a lonely-hearted flaneur.

New Orleans is a city of great bookstores. If not the veriest, then not far from it. I often spent lunch hours browsing through the Used stacks at Beckham's or lusting after a signed first edition at Octavia. The law office where I worked was located in the Quarter and a frequent stop for me was Faulkner House Books in Pirate's Alley, right across the street from Place de Henriette Delille, just a block away from Jackson Square.

One afternoon, in the late summer of 2000, I went there on my lunch break with the intention of buying the new novel of a writer whose class I'd taken while in school at Ole Miss. When I entered the shop, I nodded at the woman sitting at a desk in the back of the room where she rang up customers' purchases. For all the unbound capaciousness its floor-to-ceiling shelves of books inspired, the store itself was quite small, just one main room for the hardcover fiction and nonfiction and one ancillary hallway for poetry and drama. If there were more than a handful of customers present it could be tough to navigate without the insistent feeling that you were either in someone's way or they in yours.

On this day there was only one other customer browsing. I took little notice of her and for some time she was only an undefined presence in my periphery. Even when I had a book in mind, I always skimmed everything in the store. I'd run the index finger of my right hand along the spines of books on a shelf—I liked the feel of the different jacket covers on my fingertip, the physical connection with each book—and would stop when I found one that piqued my interest. This day I took my time, proceeding alphabetically, and after fifteen minutes or so when I got to the Hs, where my former teacher's book was, I found my path blocked by the other customer.

"Excuse me," I said, and for the first time I really took notice of her. She was in profile, eyes scanning lines in the book held open in her hands. She was short, barely five feet I'd have guessed, and thin. I remember thinking I could have easily wrapped my hand around the thickest part of her arm. There was an elegant dishevelment

14

about her. She had olive skin and long black hair that she wore piled on her head in a manner somewhat messy, as though put up just after waking, still a touch logy. It was not yet Labor Day, still sauna-like in the afternoons and syrupy in the evenings, and she wore a white dress that fit her petite figure snuggly. Upon the blank canvas of her outfit was one bit of color: a small obsidian gem that hung from a thin silver necklace. It fell just below the neckline and if I hadn't been paying closer attention, I might have thought it an ink stain.

"Excuse me," I said again.

Finally, she looked up, wrested from the world of the book.

"Oh, pardon."

Her irises were not brown or hazel; they were amber, un-human, like the eyes of an owl or fish. For a few moments neither of us said anything, staring at one another, until I told her I was looking for a book in this section and instead of moving she asked the author's name.

When I answered, she said, "You don't want to read that," and pulled it from the shelf, looking at the cover. "This is a *terrible* novel."

"My friend wrote it," I said immediately, the words jumping from my mouth before I fully knew what they meant.

Why did I say that, this lie? Was it an attempt to concatenate myself more firmly to another's achievement by suggesting an intimacy with my former teacher that was patently false, a young person's wish to attach himself to another's greatness? Or perhaps it was my instinct to mount a more compelling defense of her rebuke. How dare she criticize my friend's novel? Whatever the case, she was unmoved: "Well you should tell your friend to write a better book next time."

"I'll decide for myself," I said, taking it from her. I started to move away, my skin stippling in irritation.

"You should read this instead," she said, offering the book in her hand. It was Flaubert's *Three Tales*. I was versed enough to know Gustav Flaubert was someone I should know, but I'd never read him, knew nothing about him, and if I'd attempted to speak his name, I'd have pronounced it *flau-burt* instead of *flow-bare*. She added: "I reread it every year."

"How many times have you read it?"

"Are you trying to find out my age?"

A different kind of woman would have winked or smiled, but she didn't. She just stared back at me. I was having trouble reading this interaction. Her tone had been brusque initially but now was friendly—perhaps even flirty—and through it all her face was expressionless. It was as if I was speaking to two women who happened to be embodied in one person. Before I could respond, she asked my name and I told her.

"Dixon," she said, taking my hand in hers, "I'm Pelin." After a few moments, much to my surprise, she added: "Would you like to have lunch with me?"

"When?"

"Now."

I hadn't yet eaten. My sandwich was in the breakroom fridge, waiting for me beneath the crisp fold of a brown paper bag.

"I'm sorry, but I have to get back to work."

"I see. May I walk with you then?"

"I guess."

"Good. Now buy your novel and let's go."

After I made my purchase, we walked in the direction of my office. For a while we were silent. I felt awkward and wasn't sure what to say, or what to make of this woman. I was a little annoyed even; I had a half hour more of my lunch break left, but in an effort to remove myself from the conversation I'd lied and said I needed to get back to work. Now that she'd insisted on walking with me, I felt I had to go back to the office early.

She asked where I worked and I told her.

"You're too young to be a lawyer," she said. "Paralegal?"

"I answer phones and pick up dry cleaning."

"You want to be a lawyer though?"

She spoke with the traces of an accent I couldn't place. Something vaguely European.

"Not hardly. This is temporary."

"Until what? What is it you wish to do with yourself?"

Her probing felt invasive. I didn't want to tell her about graduate school, about wanting to be a photographer, so I told her something that I thought might smooth over an abrupt change of subject. She was obviously an avid reader; I decided to tell her about my sly game at the office, how I put chapters of books in clients' charts.

"No," she said excitedly and placed a hand on my arm. I stopped walking and turned to her, expecting to find her smiling, but still her face was blank. Now I thought I'd misread her timbre or tone and perhaps she was scolding me. She took her hand away and started walking again, nodding. Soon we were at the office, standing a few feet from the entrance. "Well," I said, gesturing toward the building, "I should get back to reading." I thought she might laugh, but she didn't even smile. She just nodded again.

"It's been nice to meet you, Dixon." She went through her purse and pulled out a book. "Here, this is for you." It was the one she'd been reading in the bookstore. I hadn't seen her pay. "I think you'll like it. Especially the story 'A Simple Heart.'"

"Did you steal this?"

"Shhh," she said, looking over her shoulder conspiratorially. "I liberated this great work of literature from captivity, and you read on the clock at work. We are keepers of the other's transgression."

She didn't say goodbye, just walked away. I watched her for a few moments, then went inside, a little confused by our interaction. The office was busy that afternoon, so I didn't have much time to think about it, but at the end of the day, as I packed up my things and cleared off my desk, I took the copy of *Three Tales* she'd stolen and stared at the cover, then flipped it over to read the back matter. I placed it in my messenger bag and walked back to Faulkner House Books. When I entered, the same woman who'd been working earlier was sitting in the exact same spot, doing what she'd been doing, as if the four hours between this very moment and then had been erased.

"I'm sorry," I said, walking toward her and taking the book from my bag. "I was in here earlier and my friend accidentally left without paying for this."

"Mrs. Ozols?"

"I'm not sure."

"You don't know your friend's last name?"

"Her name is Pelin," I said.

"That's Mrs. Ozols. She's my best customer."

"Well, she forgot to pay for this, so I'm returning it."

"She paid. Earlier. Before you entered the store."

"I see," I said. "I guess I misunderstood."

The woman slid a bookmark behind the cover, handed it back, and told me to enjoy.

I returned home, embarrassed and a little angry. Why had she lied to me? I knew nothing about Pelin, and she little of me, and yet I felt setup, as though she knew I'd try to return the book and look silly for doing so. I took it out of my bag and tossed it in the corner of my bedroom like a dirty garment. I stared at it. I imagined ripping out pages at random and making word poetry from the wreckage, but that was rash and ridiculous, so I picked it up and returned it to my bag, deciding I'd donate it to the library.

The next day, despite the heat, I sat outside on a bench near the law firm during my lunch break. Usually I tried to find a shaded spot in the park or by the river, away from the office. Sometimes I even returned to my apartment, since it was a short walk, but this day I didn't. I ate the same thing I always did, a peanut butter sandwich with raspberry jam, which always left me tonguing around the inside of my mouth in the afternoons, trying to dislodge the small crunchy seeds nestled between teeth. I tried reading as I ate but had trouble focusing. I would go for a sentence or two, then find myself looking up to see who was walking toward me on the street. I recognized no one. After work, I walked back to Faulkner House Books. There were no other customers there.

"How do you like the book?" asked the woman behind the desk.

"Which one?"

"The Flaubert."

For a moment I didn't know what she meant, but soon I understood, taking note to remember the correct pronunciation of the name.

"It's excellent, thank you."

"Can I help you find something?"

"No," I said and left the store without explanation.

I followed the same pattern the next several days before I went back to my normal routine. The following week, as I was in the midst of a fruitful spell of picture-taking, I left work one evening, happy to return home and develop some photographs I'd taken the previous night, when I saw her standing on the sidewalk across the street from the office. Pelin. Again, she was wearing white, trousers and a blouse this time, but her hair was down instead of up, much longer than I'd realized. We met eyes and she raised her hand, though it just stayed in the air before her, still, un-waving. For a moment it seemed not that she was saying hello so much as she was telling me to stop.

"Were you waiting for me?" I asked as I moved across the street and joined her.

"How are you, Dixon?"

"I'm busy."

"Busy with what?"

I could feel my shirt already starting to dampen, my neck and underarms wet. I unbuttoned the cuffs of my dress shirt and rolled them to the elbow.

"Work."

"Aren't you done with work now? How about you join me for a drink?"

"I can't."

I began to walk and she followed.

"Do you not drink? Tea then?"

"I drink. I just can't. I need to go home. I have things I need to do."

My strides were longer, and she quickened her pace to keep up.

"Where is home?" she asked.

"The Marigny."

"That's nice. I live in the Garden District."

As we walked, I took a quick look at her. Her nose was large, almost too large for a woman, a man's nose, and there were no lines on her mouth or forehead. It was like the skin below her cheeks had never been touched.

"Have you started the book I gave you?" she asked.

"I gave it away," I said, which wasn't true. The book was sitting in the ever-growing stack of I-Want-to-Read near my bed. She stopped walking and for a few beats I kept on. I could have left her there and been done with her, but I stopped and turned back.

"You are angry with me," she said. "Why?"

"I'm not angry with you. I don't even know you."

"Why are you being rude?"

"Why did you lie to me?"

"How did I lie to you?"

"You said you'd stolen the book, but you didn't. The woman at the bookstore told me you bought it before I arrived."

"Why did you talk to her about me?"

She took a step forward, nodding once.

"I went back to pay for it."

"Why?"

"Because I'm a regular there. I didn't want to be associating with thieves."

Associating with thieves? I could hear how preposterous I sounded, but she didn't laugh. She took another step, nodding once again. We were nearly out of the Quarter, the streets less crowded with people and automobiles, the air less clouded by the smell of urine and street wash, the detritus of the city's eternal bacchanal. I began to walk again, and I could hear her tiny footsteps quickening to keep up. She started telling me about the book she was reading—a novel that was getting attention for being the rare work that managed to satisfy both the high-art literati and general masses—giving a razor-sharp critique of its many faults while acknowledging its few merits. It was impressive, her casual authority. I listened intently, saying little, and was so preoccupied that I walked right past my apartment and had to turn around.

"It's beautiful," she said, taking in the building. "Goodbye, Dixon. Thank you for the walk. Have a good evening."

I started to enter but turned back.

"You were right," I said.

"About what?"

"The book I bought last week. It wasn't very good."

"Your friend's novel?"

"He's not my friend."

"No?"

"He was my teacher. I took his class in college. I don't know why I said that."

"So we both lied to each other. Innocent lies. White lies."

She was right, though I didn't say so.

"What class?" she asked.

"What do you mean?"

"What class did you take from the man who wrote the bad novel?"

"It was a writing workshop. Fiction."

"Ah, now it makes sense. You are a writer."

"No, I take pictures."

"A photographer?"

It sounded strange coming from her mouth, the title unearned. It made me uneasy, like I might be asked to produce a business card that said so.

"I just dabble," I said.

"This is what you are so busy with."

I nodded.

"I see. Then I will leave you to your work."

I thought of the pictures I'd taken the previous night: wide shots of the winding Mississippi in the lambent dusk, low-angle close-ups of smile-drunk revelers sharing stories at a bar in the Irish Channel. Already they had become less exciting to me in the space of a few minutes, and suddenly I dreaded developing them, scared of what lay waiting for me in my bathroom-turned-darkroom. These anxieties weren't daily, but they weren't uncommon: Fear of the undeveloped picture, suddenly hating something I'd loved the day before, looking for any excuse not to engage with my art.

"Would you still like to have that drink?" I asked.

"You're sure?"

I opened the door and motioned inside.

"I'd love that," she said, and we began our ascent up the stairs.

My stepmother's place was a two-bedroom apartment on the top floor of an old house near Washington Square. It was rundown, but it was a perfect place to live and work. There was a bedroom with French doors that I could leave open or closed as my mood saw fit, as well as a living room with a small comfortable sofa and reading chair. There was a round table near the kitchen that could seat four if necessary—it never was—but was perfect for two. The stove was broken, so I did what little cooking I was capable of with a microwave and hotplate. I made an office out of the smaller second room, which was a glorified closet, and referred to it, affectionately, as "the cloffice." My desk was set against the wall before a window that looked out on the courtyard below. There was one small shelf filled with books and the rest I stacked neatly but precariously in tall piles that sometimes tipped over if I wasn't careful. Pinned to the wall were poor reproductions of pictures taken by some of my favorite photographers: Arbus, Friedlander, Robert Frank. When I gave Pelin a tour of the apartment, she stepped into the cloffice and said, "Be regular and orderly in your life like a bourgeois so that you may be violent and original in your work." Only much later did I know she was quoting Flaubert.

I showed her to the living room, where she took a seat on the sofa, and asked what she'd like to drink. I didn't have much besides wine and bourbon, the former came from a box and the latter was a small rung up from bottom shelf, though I neglected to say so. She crossed her legs, thinking a moment, and said she'd like wine. I went to the kitchen, which was visible from where she sat and took out a couple of small glasses—I didn't have stemware—and filled one with Early Times, my back facing her. I took the other glass and opened the refrigerator—I knew the door, when open, would block her view—and surreptitiously filled it with wine. The bladder was almost empty, and I had to tilt the box forward to get anything to come out. When I returned, she noticed my glass.

"Bourbon," she said. "No ice?"

"I don't want anything coming between me and this whiskey."

It was something my father used to say and Pelin let out that small sound of amusement, but she didn't smile. In fact, her expression had not changed, though the tenor and tone of our interaction had softened into something pleasant. I wasn't angry or irritable anymore. I was amiably uncertain as to what was transpiring and why but willing to go along with it.

I raised my glass to hers and met eyes before taking a sip. I started to say something that felt moderately brave, that she was the first person I'd invited into my apartment in two years of living there. However, as I made this admission, Pelin began to cough. She hadn't heard what I'd said, and the moment was lost. She looked at her glass.

"Where does this wine come from? Missouri?"

"A box," I admitted after a beat of hesitation.

"My goodness," she said. "You should have warned me. What kind of bourbon are you drinking? Maybe I'll try that."

When I told her it was Early Times, she sat silent, clearly considering whether it was preferable to drink water than endure my lowly offerings. But then I recalled something one of my teachers said offhandedly in a Southern Literature class. I told her that Early Times had been Walker Percy's favorite bourbon, that he'd even written an essay about it.

"And what did Mr. Percy say?" she asked

"He said that bourbon did for him what cake did for Proust."

Pelin liked that and, with Percy's endorsement, she said she would like to try it. "But with ice, please," she added before rising and asking where the bathroom was. I pointed to a door at the other end of the room and then went about fixing her drink. When she returned, again assuming her spot on the couch, I handed her the glass and we toasted once more. After taking a sip, she said, "I tend to drink scotch when I'm in the mood for brown liquor, but this isn't bad."

We sat quietly for a few moments, a silence made salient by the fact that we were unknown to one another and shouldn't have had trouble finding things to discuss. Slowly and carefully, I turned the glass in my hands, watching the level rise and fall. I wasn't sure what was happening, what might be expected of me, and suddenly regretted having invited her in.

"Well," I said finally, "I should probably get back to—"

"You want to know something?"

"Okay."

"Whenever I used to visit the home of a man I liked for the first time, do you know what I did?"

I shook my head.

"I'd ask to use the bathroom, whether I needed to or not, and I'd lift up the toilet seat."

"Why on earth would you do that?"

"Because I wanted to see if he was a man who paid attention to things unseen and whether he cared enough to clean up after himself." She paused. "The underside of your toilet seat was spotless."

Never had I felt such relief at my fastidiousness, a trait often risible to others.

"What if it hadn't been?" I said. "Would you have left?"

I don't know how to explain or account for the physics of it, but after I said this, she looked at me with such meaning and intention that it was like she lifted me out of my chair with the power of her eyes alone—those incredible, un-human eyes—and suddenly I was walking toward her. She uncrossed her legs as I knelt before her.

"I don't know," she said, leaning forward, bringing her face within inches of mine. "Would you have let me?"

The question ignited something in me, a courage and understanding absent previously, and then I was kissing her.

*

As we lay in bed that first evening in my apartment, I wondered if this had been her intent all along, from the first time we met in the bookstore, and asked her if that was the case.

"What?" she said.

Then I realized the real question I was wanting to ask.

"Why me?"

It seemed to confuse her, though her face was blank as a manikin's, and suddenly she grew angry: "You want me to explain desire and instinct? We are animals. Isn't that enough?"

"I'm sorry. I didn't mean to upset you. It's just…"

"What?"

"I have trouble reading you. Your face reveals nothing."

"Dixon—"

"You'd make a great gambler. We should go to the casino."

I smiled at her and she stared back, expressionless.

"See!" I cried. "You're incredible."

"Stop it." She looked away.

"What?"

"It's not a joke. I have a condition."

She explained that she had a nervous disorder that left her unable to show affect. She could emote, but the accompanying facial expression never manifested. When she laughed, sound emitted from her throat, but her face remained unchanged. When she cried, water fell from her eyes down still cheeks. Suddenly, much of my confusion about the awkwardness of our encounters made sense.

"You'll know when I'm smiling though," she said.

"How?"

"Because I nod my head."

"And you shake it when you're unhappy?"

"Correct. When I'm sad."

I'd never heard of such a thing. I started to apologize but stopped myself. It didn't seem so much an affliction to express regret over as much as a reality that made her lived experience unordinary. It was, as she said, a condition. She was lying next to me with her head on my chest and one leg snaked over mine, but suddenly she moved atop me. She looked down from above and began to slide back and forth over my middle until I felt the stirrings once again. "This one," she said, grabbing her left breast, "is more sensitive than the other. When I'm about to come I want you to squeeze it hard." She stopped moving and without breaking eye contact leaned forward, close to my face, as she reached between her legs and slipped me inside her. We inhaled deeply, simultaneously, and she began to move slowly, undulant, whole-bodied.

The first time we had sex she hadn't come—I hadn't given her time to—but this time the approach of her climax was unmistakable. When it arrived, I reached for her left breast, squeezed it a little, then plucked the nipple hard between thumb and forefinger, and she made a deafening sound that could have been mistaken for screams of terror. Her entire body shook, like someone undergoing exorcism, and I worried my downstairs neighbors might think an assault was occurring. I grew to love her earsplitting orgasms, but that first time surprised and unsettled me, taking me out of the moment. After her shriek faded, she collapsed on my chest and I wrapped my arms around her tightly as her body quivered with little tremors and aftershocks.

Imagine the incongruity: to hear that sound emit from a face as blank as fine tablecloth.

*

We made plans to meet at my place the following evening after I got off work, and when Pelin arrived she was holding a bouquet of flowers and a bottle of clear liquor. Housewarming gifts, she called them, though I'd been living there for two years. "Tiger lilies," she said, handing them to me. "My favorite flowers. Aren't they gorgeous?" They were. The petals were spotted orange, like their namesake. I inhaled the flowers' strong and sweet scent before looking in the cabinets for a vase but couldn't find one, so I placed them in the blender with a little water from the tap. "If you're going to be a tortured artist," said Pelin as she handed me the bottle, "you should at least have decent alcohol. You're going to need it."

"Who said anything about being tortured?" I studied the bottle. I'd assumed it was vodka at first, but I realized it was a liqueur. I remembered her last name, Ozols, which sounded Greek, so I ventured, "Ouzo?"

"No," she said forcefully, as if I might have offended her. "Raki. From Turkey, not Greece."

"I thought maybe since your last name was—"

"Ozols is my husband's name. It's Latvian."

It was the first time her husband had been invoked, though his specter was always present in the form of her large, glistering engagement ring. The beautiful object would forever function as a synecdoche of their life together, as well as my exclusion from it.

"Does your husband know you're here?"

"There are many things Rostyk knows and some he doesn't. This he does not know."

It wasn't so much guilt I was feeling as curiosity. I wondered of the mental gymnastics one must undertake to betray a beloved. Of course, I was no innocent in the matter, but I also wasn't the one who was married.

"Do you love him?"

"Yes."

"Would he be upset that you're here?"

She gave me a look—with her eyes alone—that made me feel dim for thinking he might feel otherwise.

"What does Rostyk do?"

"He works with boats in the port."

"A dockworker?"

She began to laugh one of her expressionless laughs that looked vaguely epileptic: her face completely still as her chest earthquaked. It always unsettled me to see her like that. Though I tried not to let on, I worried she sensed it, my discomfort in a moment she was happy.

"Are you kidding? He's not some roustabout walking the pier with a knit hat, hook in hand, like *On the Waterfront*. He's sitting in a skyscraper downtown on the phone with somebody in Japan." She paused, touching my arm. "He owns a shipping company."

I'd assumed Pelin had money—her style of dress, her seemingly free days, her home in the Garden District, and above all the way she carried herself, comfortable in her privilege—but the source of it was a question too gauche to ask. Now I was starting to understand. Rostyk had been born in Riga, she told me, and made his fortune running shipping routes through the Baltic after the collapse of the USSR. They'd been married eight years and she reiterated that she cared for him very much. Actually, what she reiterated was that she loved him, but Rostyk was older and worked long days. A familiar enough story: there was little passion left for her, she said, but they were good companions and friends.

"Fifteen years is a significant age difference," she said, and suddenly my brain was awash in figures, trying to do the math. Pelin was thirty-three, ten years older than I was, and Rostyk was fifteen years older than she. He was, I realized, my father's age. I asked another question about her husband, but she waved it off— "Enough about Rostyk"—and turned our attention to the bottle. "We need two small glasses."

I went to the cupboard and removed the smallest ones I could find, juice glasses.

"Perfect," she said. She brought the raki over to the kitchen counter. "You have chilled water?"

"I have tap water."

"I see."

She went to the freezer, poked her head inside, and returned with a half-filled ice tray from which she selected two cubes and dropped one into each glass. Then she opened the bottle of raki and filled each halfway before topping it off with a splash of cold water from the tap. She set the glasses on the counter again and we watched them begin to cloud a milky-white, like the emulsifying louche effect I'd seen a few times at bars in the Quarter when the bartender added water to absinthe.

"Lion's milk," said Pelin. She handed one glass to me and held the other against her ribs, as though her hand were lame.

"What shall we toast to?"

"In Turkey, my father and his friends say, 'anani sikerim.'"

"What does it mean?"

"Motherfucker," she said, a little embarrassed. This was the first and only time I heard her curse in English; she reserved swearing for her first language. "Technically, it means, 'I have intercourse with your mother.'"

"Charming."

"My father has charming friends."

It took me a moment to realize she'd made a joke. Her face, as always, betrayed nothing. The effect was not unlike someone wearing a mask of her own likeness, and sometimes I imagined she might one day take it off so I could see her true face. She said the words again—*anani sikerim*—and I repeated them, but she stopped me when I tried to clink her glass with the rim of mine. "We toast from the bottom in Turkey." I followed her lead and then raised the glass to my nose. I could smell the aniseed, the plumb and grape, and then I took a small amount into my mouth, letting it rest on my tongue a moment before it burned a quick trail down my throat.

I was curious about her past, about Turkey, and when I asked, she told me she'd been born in Istanbul but was raised largely in Switzerland and later France. Her parents were college professors at Istanbul Technical University. Progressive Muslims who embraced the West, they sent their daughter to a boarding school in Romandy, the French-speaking part of Switzerland, and later to study in Burgundy. Pelin's unique accent and tough-to-pin-down pan-Europeanism made more sense now.

"And you?" she said. "Tell me about where you grew up."

"Born and raised in Mississippi. There's not much to tell."

"Yes, there is. I can see by your discomfort at the question."

I hadn't noticed a change in my comportment, but that she had perturbed me a little.

"It's just…I don't really." I paused. "Another time I will."

"Okay, another time then," she said, looking away from me, "but I'm going to hold you to it."

Her gaze fell upon a stack of prints I'd developed earlier in the week.

"How is it coming, your photography?"

Quickly I turned them over.

"Slowly."

"What are you working on?"

"I'm trying to find the pictures that will make up my application portfolio for grad school. They can't just be good. They must be excellent."

"I would love to see your work. Perhaps I could help you decide what to include."

"I couldn't do that," I said.

"Why not? I'm a good critic. I'll be honest."

"That's what scares me."

I thought of the way she'd so convincingly extemporized a critique of the best-selling novel on our walk the day before and could hardly imagine showing her my pictures. I knew that her approbation would have meant everything to me, while her disfavor would have crushed me.

"Please show me, Dixon," she said, nodding. Her condition was still new to me and I struggled to remember a nod of her head signified a smile.

"I'm not ready yet," I said. "But I will."

"Promise?"

"Yes."

"That's two promises you've made to me today," she said. "I'm keeping track."

I took another sip of the raki. It was strong. I liked that it necessitated you drink it slowly.

"Well, if you're not going to tell me about your childhood and you're not going to talk about your photographs, tell me something about you that I don't know."

"There's so much. Where to begin?"

"Anywhere."

29

I thought a few moments, but my mind went blank as it often does when put on the spot. I was preparing to change the subject when something surfaced that I thought she might find interesting. "Feel this," I said, placing her hand on my right forearm. She rubbed it back and forth over the smooth and hairless skin and wrapped her hand around it. "Now feel the left." She moved her hand to the other forearm and her eyebrows raised, though the rest of her face remained still.

"It's twice as big, yes?"

"From tennis."

I explained that I'd played for many years and my left hand had gotten stronger and bigger than my right because I was left-handed on the forehand side, and furthermore, I hit a one-handed backhand, so my right hand got little use while my left was constantly engaged while playing. This sometimes happened to tennis players, I told her. Rod Laver was famous for having one normal-sized forearm and one that looked like an Easter ham.

"When did you start playing?" she asked.

"When I was young. First or second grade. Which for a kid in rural Mississippi was something of a novelty. All the other boys played football or baseball. Basketball. But being into tennis was something else, like saying I loved ice hockey or cricket." She nodded, encouraging me to continue my story. "But I kept playing and eventually even my parents came to see it wasn't a waste of time. They signed me up for lessons and later I had a coach. I played in tournaments throughout the region and eventually became quite good. That's how I ended up at Ole Miss. On a tennis scholarship."

"You are an athlete," she said, intrigued, and looked me up and down as if examining my carriage for confirmation. It felt good that I could surprise her, that there were parts of myself she hadn't yet sussed out, which I could choose to reveal or not to reveal to her.

"Was," I said. "I *was* an athlete."

"You no longer play?"

I shook my head, but she didn't ask why, perhaps because the answer was commonplace and rather boring: I'd fallen out of love with the sport once it came to feel like a job.

"So, you were an athlete," she said. "And a great one at that if you played in college."

"Greatness is so variable." I thought a moment. "Maybe I was a certain kind of great. A lesser kind. For example, I think it's safe to say I was a better tennis player than ninety-five percent of the people on the planet. But the distance between me and the last of that final five percent, that place where the best professionals like Sampras and Agassi live, is like the distance between here and Pluto. It is so beyond comprehension as to be meaningless. It takes a lesser greatness to understand that kind of true greatness. Otherwise, it's impossible. It's like trying to fathom what a million dollars is when you make fifteen grand a year."

She nodded, and I suddenly felt foolish, realizing I'd just used this analogy in conversation with someone who likely knew exactly what a million dollars looked and felt like.

"And how does this relate to photography, your tennis?" she asked. "What happened to you in Oxford?"

I told her that in college I'd been drawn to the literature offerings and became an English major, deciding I wanted to be a writer, though at first I was mostly in love with the idea of being a writer. I hung out at Square Books, got drunk at City Grocery, recounted apocryphal Barry Hannah and Larry Brown stories as if I'd been present when they might have happened. I fantasized I was Faulkner as I walked the grounds of Rowan Oak and made late-night pilgrimages to his grave, where I'd drink from a pint of Four Roses and leave it on his headstone as visitors sometimes do, an offering to the master.

"You were a poseur," she said, sliding into the French that would come out occasionally.

"Yes." I took another sip of the raki. "Worse, despite my love of reading and a strong desire to write, I discovered I wasn't any good at it. I mean truly not good."

"I'm sure you weren't that bad."

"My professor once responded to a story I'd written by taping a matchstick to the final page. That's how bad I was."

I laughed and she nodded.

"That's when I knew my short-lived career as a writer was over."

"What did you do?" she asked.

"I dropped the class and picked up another that sounded easy. Photography 101. I knew nothing about cameras, nothing about making pictures. None of the history or theory. I don't think I even thought of it as art at the time. It was just something people did to document an occasion."

"And this class changed that."

"It changed my life. I quit the tennis team. I sold my racket to a used sporting-goods store and bought an old Minolta 35 millimeter."

"Do you miss it, tennis?"

"No. But I'll always be grateful for the experience. For a long time, these two passions seemed to have little to do with one another, tennis and photography, but I see it now, their connection. If I do make it as an artist, it'll be because my time as an athlete prepared me for it. The discipline and routine. The effort."

"But what about talent? It plays no part?"

"Of course, it does. It's just—"

"You have no control over it."

"Exactly."

"And this scares you, I can see." She stared at me, but I neither confirmed nor denied it. Finally, she said, "That's very interesting," and I could tell she meant it by the way she looked pensively into space for a moment. Soon she would tell me she had to leave. Despite the passion of the previous day, neither of us made a move toward physical intimacy. There was nothing awkward about it, no sense of regret for what we'd done. It simply didn't come up; we were too busy talking, too busy getting to know one another.

*

We began seeing each other regularly, for a little over an hour, after I got off work before she returned home for the evening. When she arrived, I was often sitting in the cloffice looking over photographs I'd developed the previous night. She'd come toward me and I'd feel her hand on my shoulder, then a kiss on my neck, as she leaned close to catch a glimpse, but before she could see anything I'd rise and usher her out to the main room.

We would have sex, tremendous sex, but just as arousing were our conversations. I left our encounters with lists of books that I needed to read, films I needed to see, music I needed to hear. That was how she always phrased her recommendations—as a need, never that

I should—which made them feel more than mere suggestions. I remember checking out a film she recommended from the library. "You need to see this, Dixon," she'd said. But after I watched it, when I told her how much I loved Herzog's *Aguirre, The Wrath of God*, I'd mistakenly pronounced the title character's name *Ag-wire* and she'd corrected me: "Uh-*gee*-ray, dear." She didn't mean it hurtfully, but my lack of cultivation shamed me, my callowness and roots in rural Mississippi. There were other instances like this, moments when Pelin would assert her authority or expose, not unkindly, my unknowingness. I knew how to correctly pronounce Mann and Proust, but who knows what might have come out of my mouth if forced to say the names of Goethe and Gide. She knew so much more than I about the world to which I longed entrance.

My job had always been something to be endured, unrewarding labor that was simply a means to a paycheck, but now I even struggled for the concentration it took to slack off on duty. While trying to covertly read, my mind wandered to Pelin and I'd spend tortuous afternoons at the office, warm and fidgety with desire, willing the second hand on the clock to spin faster so that five p.m. would arrive and I could punch out and leave.

Before Pelin, I hadn't slept with anyone in my two years in New Orleans, and I'd only ever had one serious, long-term relationship, one that swallowed up the majority of my college years. Her name was Sara and she played tennis on Auburn University's women's team. We'd met at the conference championships our freshman year and struck up a long-distance relationship that saw me logging long hours in the car between Oxford and Auburn, and despite this we'd made it work for almost three years. She was pretty and smart and kind, but something changed when I quit playing tennis after my junior year. We'd lost a common love that had been the conduit through which our lives converged, and we decided, with no acrimony, to break up.

All of which is to say, I was not sexually practiced—or at least not widely—and my relationship with Pelin was an education in many ways, sentimental and otherwise. I might have longed to go to graduate school to study photography, but she was right then, at that moment, already providing an impeccable tutelage of erotics.

*

One afternoon—this would have been in mid-October, when the summer heat had finally broken—the phone on my desk at work rang. I picked it up immediately. I'd learned to do so after being scolded by one of the partners in the firm who'd had to wait six rings for me to answer.

"Surprise," said the voice in my ear.

"Pelin," I said, indeed surprised. She'd never called me at work. "Is everything okay?"

My alarm provoked in her a light laugh, but it was also a refracted pleasure with herself, her covert mischief. In my mind's eye, I pictured her smiling, even though I'd never seen her do so, even though it was an impossibility.

"Imagine I am under your desk and taking you in my mouth as you talk to your boss. You must not let him know what is happening."

I looked around the office. There were a couple of paralegals nearby, heads in files.

"I can't talk now," I said.

Again, she laughed.

"That's fine. I will talk for us."

She told me that today she would not be coming over to my apartment after work. My heart sunk a little until she said we would do something special instead. Rostyk was out of town on business; tonight we would have dinner and go to the ballet. I was excited by the prospects. While I loved our evenings together, it did sadden me that our relationship seemed to exist only within the small confines of my stepmother's apartment. She told me to dress well, that she'd arrive in a cab to pick me up at six-thirty sharp.

That night I donned my lone suit, which was made of gray wool. I'd bought it in a second-hand shop in Oxford and it fit me perfectly. It was a bit heavy for the weather, but I felt good wearing it as I accompanied Pelin with her bright silver minaudiere into Galatoire's, where we were seated and attended to by a team of servers. I felt like an imposter but also a gentleman. Though she usually wore white, whatever the season, that night Pelin wore a black silk dress with a thin pink ribbon that wound round the waist. The restaurant—which I'd never been to and couldn't have possibly afforded on my own without making a significant dent in my savings for graduate school—was crowded and loud, something I normally would have loathed, but I didn't mind having to raise my voice to be heard or having to say excuse me to the man whose chair I backed into when I rose too quickly to find the bathroom. Pelin ordered for me and we feasted on delicious dishes I'd never tasted before—escargot, turtle soup, sweetbreads, and bouillabaisse—while splitting a bottle of Langlois Brut Rose. I made no pretense of reaching for the check. I understood this night to be a special gift from Pelin, and I felt comfortable accepting. After the bill was paid, she raised her glass, and the splash of wine that remained in it, and said, "To you, my passion."

It was the first time I remember her calling me that, her passion, which became a favorite term of endearment.

"To us," I said, and took a sip from my glass before I realized it was empty and set it down.

I'd never been to the ballet and when I thought of it at all, I recalled watching a performance of *The Nutcracker* on Public Television—one of three channels we got if you bent the tin foil on the rabbit ears of the TV just right—as a boy during the holiday season. It had not prepared me for what we saw that night, which was a series of discrete dances performed by a duo set to the music of a contemporary Hungarian composer. The stage was barren, no props, so the dancers had plenty of room to move. The female dancer, who was white, was wearing a pale pink slip and white tights, and the male dancer, who was Black, wore only loose black bottoms. She was petite and he was taller, his body and limbs lithe and muscular as Greek statuary. He lifted her easily, spun her slowly in the air to the music's melancholy register, then slowly let her slide down his chest. I was transfixed. They were beautiful together, and though they never so much as kissed, I felt I was seeing perhaps the most erotic thing I'd ever witnessed.

Afterward, on the cab ride back to my place, I told Pelin just that.

"You didn't know ballet could be like that, did you?"

"I want to see more," I said. "Do you go often?"

"Not as much as I used to."

"Why?"

I had sensed a faint sadness or remove come over her once we left dinner but had said nothing in the theater once I was under the spell of the dancers. Perhaps the night's splendor had been tarnished by the awareness we couldn't do this whenever we liked.

"I used to dance," she said. "In fact, I danced with her, that woman we just watched, many years ago."

"What?"

"Can you believe she's forty-two? This is her final year dancing."

I was shocked. I had so many questions, but they manifested in silence. I was relieved when she continued:

"My parents started me early, when I was in Turkey, and I continued to dance in Switzerland and then in France. That's why I moved there. I was the youngest ballerina in the company. My whole life I danced, up until I was twenty-five, shortly after I met Rostyk. He was in Paris on business when he saw me perform and afterward insisted on meeting me." I set my hand on her leg. "I would have liked to continue dancing, but I injured my ankle and my body couldn't take it anymore after so many years. Soon we married, and I left that life behind to come here."

While I felt no desire to play tennis any longer, it wouldn't have pained me in the least to watch it, as I occasionally did, but I could see it wasn't the same for Pelin. It wounded her in a way she found difficult to talk about. While I'd left the sport voluntarily, she'd been forced to retire. Stupidly, I tried to cheer her up, my tone becoming jovial and chummy: "See, you were an athlete, too—we do make quite the pair."

She looked at me. Inscrutable, that face.

"No, my passion. I wasn't an athlete," she said. "I was an artist."

*

I took the GREs in mid-October and found out my scores a week or two later. For all my months of study, the vocab flashcards and practice tests, the revisiting of old math equations I hadn't seen since high school, I did merely average, as I always had on standardized tests. My brain simply doesn't work that way. I did very well in school, but I needed the space and time a semester of study provided, not a couple of hours filling in bubbles on a blue scantron sheet. But it didn't really matter. I'd later learn that the test was a formality. I was applying to what were then considered the five preeminent art programs in the country, and what would decide my fate was not my test scores but my portfolio. I didn't have internet access, let alone a computer, in the apartment, so I'd written the schools directly, asking them to send applications via post. Patiently, I filled them out, composed my personal statement, tracked down letters of reference and transcripts, wrote checks for the application fees. I stacked them neatly beside my desk in the cloffice. The only thing left to do was finalize my portfolio. I'd abandoned the pictures I'd been favoring before I met Pelin and begun taking new ones that I was starting to feel good about, ones I thought might even meet her high aesthetic standards. I was making progress and felt confident that by the end of November I'd be ready to submit my applications.

*

A fact many residents of New Orleans must face is the sheer number of people, persistent to the point of self-invitation, who want to come visit whether you'd like them to or not. I was lucky in this regard. Aside from my stepmother, who wasn't really a guest since it was her apartment, I hadn't had a single visitor in my two years, at least until that fall when a former teammate of mine from Ole Miss wrote to say he was coming. His name was Judson Haus, or as he was more commonly known on the team, "Brick House," because he looked like he should have been on the offensive line of the football team instead of playing doubles for us. When I began to fall out of love with the game, my play slipped, and our coach moved me from playing singles to doubles, and for a time, while Judson's regular partner recovered from an elbow injury, he and I were partners. I loved playing with him. We were the odd couple. While I was reserved, on and off the court, he was an absolute maniac when we played, cracking humorous asides one moment, taunting our opponents the next, and arguing with the chair umpire on changeovers. Despite his size, he was deceptively quick—he had small feet that gave him a hurried Babe Ruth-style canter—and a monster forehand. When he'd pancake the ball hard and flat, I imagined flames coming off the yellow felt and pitied our opponent at the net as he steeled himself to volley.

We maintained a friendship after I quit the team and had even carried on sporadic correspondence—with him sending me humorous postcards in response to my lengthy and overly earnest letters—in the years after graduation. One day that fall, I received a postcard from him that simply said: *For the love of God, Dixie, check your email account once in a while.* I'd gone to college without having ever used email and rarely checked it anymore, especially after graduation, but when I received Judson's note I went to an internet café and spent two hours going through a few months of email until I found Judson's, the subject line of which was: *Get Ready to Show Your Titties in the Quarter.* Oh lord, I thought, knowing what lay before me.

Judson was planning to pass through town on his way home to Baton Rouge to visit his family for Thanksgiving. He wanted to come early so he could spend a few days with me. He proposed staying four, but I talked him down to two, claiming, with some legitimacy, that I had a deadline to submit my applications. In truth, I couldn't imagine not seeing Pelin for that long. He arrived on a Wednesday afternoon. I worked a half day and arranged to take Thursday off, saying I had a family member visiting. I'd told Pelin about Judson's visit and that we'd not be able to see each other for a few days, which she understood, the same way I did when she had something come up that disrupted our rendezvous.

Judson arrived at my door carrying a small leather duffle that he dropped to the floor. "Dixie," he said, using the nickname family members had given me in childhood that I'd mistakenly revealed to him. It was strange to hear someone other than kin call me that. He moved to give me a hug and when I thought of the image later and what we must have looked like, I saw myself being mauled by a bear. Appraising me afterward, he said, "In all my born days. Goddamn, look at you. Still just a kid. I'm balding at twenty-three. Let's have a good drunk, whadya say?"

I could smell liquor on his breath, and I imagined him driving that ribbon of Interstate-10 tossing back airplane minis in one furious gulp and throwing the empty bottles out the window. Judson had always been a big drinker—he was immune to hangovers and somehow it never affected his play on the court—and I'd expected this, had prepared myself for what was to be a night of heedless carousing. We set out for the Quarter, stopping at the corner store to purchase to-go beers for the walk—"How'd you get them to name this after you," he joked, holding up a Dixie tallboy— and afterword he told me about his recent move to Atlanta to work for an insurance firm and I told him about my time in the city, not mentioning anything about Pelin. Despite intentions to pace myself, I got drunker than I had been since college. He kept putting drinks in front of me, urging me on, for old times' sake. I'd demure and then cave. I recall little, though I know we were asked to leave a bar at one point when Judson kept trying to reach for a bottle to refill his glass himself. At some point I blacked out and woke momentarily to find myself draped over his shoulder like a large grain sack, but then I was out again, waking later to Judson shaking my shoulders, then patting my cheek. We were inside a cab. "Hey, bud. You're okay. Come back to me," he said. "Tell this guy your address, okay."

The following morning, I was miserable. I'd been sick after we got home and now felt as though I'd thrown up my Adam's apple along with the contents of my stomach. I felt hollow, like my insides had been shoveled out by a melon scooper. I'd taken three Ibuprofen and chugged a glass of water before collapsing into bed and still my head pounded, still my limbs ached with dehydration. I walked out into the living room and found Judson's ursine form covering every available inch of the sofa's surface. He wore only plaid boxers and his large, uncircumcised penis snaked out through the open fold of the crotch like one of those awful sandworm creatures from *Dune*. He must have sensed me staring at him, because his right eyelid opened, the left remaining shut, and he said, "Jesus, what happened? You look like an unmade bed."

I was already wanting him to leave, but there was still another day to be endured with this man, my old friend, whom I couldn't help but think of as my own personal Ignatius J Reilly. I decided we'd take in some sites. I took him to Café du Monde for café au lait and beignets, which he snacked on—the powdered sugar peppering his black shirt like dandruff—as we walked through the French Market. I tried to avoid bars, but he insisted we stop in

Lafitte's for a Bloody Mary. "Hair of the dog, Dixie." I watched him drink as I sipped ice water. "You want this?" he said, pulling a pickled green bean from his plastic cup. What I wanted was to get out of the Quarter, so we caught a cab to City Park, where I insisted we go to the New Orleans Museum of Art. They were running an incredible exhibition of work by African American folk artists.

An hour or so later, when we'd finished and were outside on the sidewalk, I told Judson how much I enjoyed it, enthusiastically describing several of the pieces as we walked. He nodded in agreement, saying he enjoyed it, too; however, he did so using a racial epithet. He said it so flippantly, so casually, as though it were any other kind of adjective describing an artistic style or school—"landscape" say, or "Cubist"—that I hadn't yet registered it when a guy standing nearby on the sidewalk got in Judson's face.

"What the fuck did you say, big fella?" the man said.

Judson seemed unaware that he'd said anything out of the ordinary and was confused. He tried to brush the man aside and keep walking, but he kept after us.

"Say it again," the man said. He looked to be in his forties and wore a bucket hat with the Saints logo on it. "Say the word again, big fella."

"The fuck you talking about?"

"Say it again and me and you gonna mix."

Judson simply stared at him.

"Say it, big fella, so I can ask you and your bitch-boy for a dance."

Only then did Judson seem to finally understand the nature of the encounter. I suspect that as far as he was concerned, he'd just pulled any old word from the vast storehouse of colorful Southern idiom. Like me, he'd grown up hearing Black and white people use the n-word word all the time; unlike me, he thought that gave him license to use it himself. As ludicrous as it sounds, he probably could have made a straight-faced, if unconvincing, argument that the word wasn't offensive. Were it a different situation, perhaps he might have apologized, but the point was moot: this man didn't want an apology and Judson was in no mood to issue one.

"I'll say whatever I want," said Judson, but he didn't say the word again. Instead he extended his middle finger and said, "Hey, friend, why don't you sit on this and spin?"

"You and your bitch-boy would like that, wouldnya."

"Oh we'd like that just fine."

"Say it to me. Say the word. Say it to my face. I dare you."

But Judson wouldn't. He just said he'd make "shaky pudding" out of the guy if he didn't shut up, and finally the man lost interest and let us pass. Judson threw his arm around me, brushing off the incident. "Come on, Dixie," he said. "Let's catch the streetcar." He looked back at the man. "What a loon. Just words, is all."

"We both know that's not true," I said.

Judson rolled his eyes.

"Don't give me that PC bullshit they fed us at school," he started, then stopped and thought a moment. "Okay, fine. I'm sorry. I take it back."

"But you can't."

"Hey, Dixie. Listen. Don't let's ruin our day over this. I'm fixing to have a little fun before I head home tomorrow."

If the man hadn't acknowledged me with his taunt suggesting I was Judson's catamite, I would have experienced the encounter as a total nonentity. I did nothing, said nothing, shocked into a shameful silence. I could still hear the man's voice calling after us: "I'll remember your face, big fella. I'ma find you. You and your bitch-boy."

The reminder that Judson was leaving tomorrow was a small solace, and soon the incident was behind us. We caught the streetcar on Canal and transferred at St. Charles, riding it uptown to the Garden District, where we got off and walked on Magazine, past the shops and boutiques, with Judson periodically stopping into a bar to get a roadie or snack, until eventually we came to Washington Street. I wanted to show him Lafayette Cemetery No 1, and as we passed Commander's Palace, I saw Pelin sitting on the patio having lunch with a man I could only take to be Rostyk. His back was to me, but he was wearing a handsome navy suit that made more striking and pronounced the silver of his wavy hair. I wondered what his face looked like as I paused there in the street. Instinctively I waved, forgetting myself. Pelin's eyes broke contact with Rostyk's, and she looked at me momentarily without expression and then turned her attention back to him.

"What's wrong?" said Judson. He was standing there, his hand impaling a red bag of Zapp's Crawtators.

"Nothing," I said, starting to walk again. "The cemetery is up here on the left."

When we returned to the apartment, Judson took a nap and I fiddled with my camera a bit but had trouble concentrating. Having seen him that very day, I realized that Rostyk—and thus my transgression with his wife—had until then been only an abstraction, and a guilt swelled within me, though it didn't stop me from longing for Pelin and wondering if she was upset with me for having waved. Our chance encounter that afternoon was the very reason we never went to the Garden District together. Though it was one of my favorite neighborhoods in the city, it was *her* neighborhood, and we couldn't risk being indiscreet so close to her friends, neighbors, and husband. On a whim I called her on my stepmother's land line, keeping my voice quiet. She answered on the third ring.

"Can you talk?" I said.

"Yes, there's no one here. Rostyk went back to work."

"Pelin, I'm sorry about earlier."

"Don't be, my passion."

"I didn't mean to—"

"I know you didn't," she said and the air between us went static a moment. "That mountain next to you earlier, he is your friend?"

I told her I missed her. It had only been a couple of days, but it felt much longer after towing the anvil that was my old teammate around the city. On a whim I suggested she come meet us that night. I was planning on taking Judson to hear music on Frenchman Street. She laughed at my eagerness and desperation to see her, saying soon enough, but I persisted and eventually she came around to the idea. The plan was that Judson and I would head over to the Spotted Cat around 8pm and sometime thereafter Pelin would "just happen" to bump into us.

Later that night, when Pelin entered the club, I feigned surprise at running into her. We shook hands, which was strange, as it was something we'd only done once before, back in our brief prelapsarian days, and I introduced her as a friend.

"A pleasure to meet you, Judson."

"Pleasure's all mine, ma'am," he said.

It was crowded and the music was loud—we were yelling just to make these introductions—so I suggested we go down the street to The Maison, where we found sanctuary on the second-floor balcony. Judson parted the crowd like a ship's prow through water on his way to the bar to get us drinks and for a few minutes it was just Pelin and me, alone. I tried to give her a quick kiss and she said, "Careful" as she pulled away. We turned so that we faced out over the balcony, arms resting atop the railing, elbows nestled against one another in a way that would look inadvertent to anyone else but was something much more loving and intentional to us. How good it felt to have even just one small part of her touching me.

"Your friend," she said. "He is the biggest man I've ever seen."

"You should see him try to sleep on my sofa."

She laughed in her special way at the image, and we watched the revelers pass on the street below us as the sound of music from a half dozen different clubs and street buskers comingled in the night. I liked this, our little play we were putting on for Judson, and the sexual tension it wrought, pretending we were only acquaintances. Soon he returned, somehow carrying six plastic cups.

"I got two for each of us," he said, handing us our drinks, then raising one of his own. "Cheers."

"Anani sikerim," Pelin and I said at the same time.

We'd taken to using her father's bawdy toast whenever we drank together, and I spoke without thinking. Judson looked at each of us with a bemused little smile.

"What does that mean?" he said.

I looked at Pelin.

"To your health," she said. "In Turkish."

If she'd been able to smile, I would have lost it, but I managed to keep from laughing. Like Pelin, I nodded as Judson tried to repeat the toast, unwittingly telling us that he'd had sex with our mothers.

"So how do you know each other?" he asked after we'd all touched glasses.

Such a simple, obvious question, and yet I'd not prepared a response in advance. I froze.

"We met in a bookstore," said Pelin.

Which was true. Judson looked at me, grinning, and said, "That sounds like Dixie alright," then he turned to Pelin. "He was always the one on the team bus reading while the rest of us listened to music or watched movies."

"Tell me a story about Dixon from your college days."

"I don't like where this is going," I said.

"Oh, shoot. I could tell you stories for days about this one," said Judson, throwing a paw onto my shoulder. He thought a moment. "I remember the day he quit the team. After practice he came up to a few of us who were his closest friends and made a big deal of needing to tell us something important. Okay, we said, give it to us. But he wouldn't tell us right there and then. He told us to come over to his dorm room that night."

It was true. I hadn't thought it was strange at the time not to tell everyone right away at once, because while I'd made the decision to quit the team, I hadn't yet told our coach or my girlfriend Sara about it. In my mind it was an important decision, one of the most significant of my life to that point, and there was a chain of command by which I should communicate the news.

"So when we all show up at his place later," Judson continued, "we find him sitting on his bed looking nervous as all hell. I say to him, 'What's wrong, Dixie?' and he tells us to take a seat. I'm thinking he's got major news. Someone's died or...I don't know... something bad's happened, you know. And we all find a spot to sit down and he's silent for a while, just sitting there and really looking each of us each in the eye for a few seconds."

"You're embellishing," I said.

"Nope—that's how it was. I remember it exactly. You were like a doctor getting ready to tell a patient he has a week to live."

Pelin laughed an expressionless laugh.

"So I say, 'What is it? Come out with it already.' And finally, he says it. Here I am expecting him to say he has cancer and all he says is he doesn't want to play tennis anymore, like the fate of the world depended on him doing so." Judson stopped, looking at Pelin and then at me, playing up the dramatic pause. "We were all silent for a few seconds and finally I said, 'That's it?' You don't wanna play tennis anymore?"

I suppose I'd made more of a production of it than I should have. In the solipsism of youth, I'd mistakenly thought that what felt momentous in my life would have a commensurate impact on theirs.

"The truth was," continued Judson, "I thought you were going to tell us you were light in your loafers."

"What? What do you mean?"

"I thought you were gonna tell us you were a fa—"

"I *know* what the expression means. I'm asking why you would think that?"

The tone of my question carried an edge that I regretted, but the remark caught me off guard.

"Now don't get all bowed up, Dixie. It's just, you know. You were, let's say, *u*-nique. Always reading a damn book. Quiet to the point of being aloof. You weren't like the other guys on the team."

"Did others think that?"

"Hell if I know. It's not something we talked about." He looked at Pelin. I'd almost forgotten she was there, observing our back and forth. "Lighten up, pal. Have a drink."

I tried to smile, and the moment passed. We continued talking about other matters and ventured downstairs to hear a jazz band play for a while. Soon it was time to go and Pelin took off, shaking our hands again and saying she was glad she'd run into us, and then it was just Judson and me, walking home in the opposite direction.

"My lord," he said, turning back to watch her walk in the distance. "Her pants are so tight, I can see her religion. What I wouldn't give to flick her little bean." I said nothing. Judson was that particular kind of Southern man who was supremely well mannered and deferential in situations where he was on the lesser side of an age or class disparity but stunningly and idiomatically crass around people he considered himself equal to or better than. "She's not beautiful, but she's sexy as hell. Do you know what I mean, Dixie? It's strange. I can't explain it. What do you think she was doing out here by herself anyway? She looking for company?"

"She's married," I said, the edge returning to my voice.

"I saw the asteroid on her finger, but that don't mean she's not out here fishing for dick."

"Don't," I said, but he was so worked up he didn't hear and kept going on, saying awful things. "Stop it!" I said and spun around quickly, throwing all my force into a punch that grazed off the side of his head. I'd never struck anyone and it showed. It was as though I'd tossed a pebble at him. He was unfazed, more confused than anything, staring back at me. It was both embarrassing and emboldening to act out in this way.

"What," he said, "are you *doing*?"

"I'm sorry." Quickly I tried to regain my composure. "But she's my friend. She's nice. She's a lady. Don't talk about her that way."

I started walking again and a few moments later he spoke.

"Oh, I see."

"What?"

"*You're* fucking her, aren't you?"

"Pelin? No. I told you, we're just friends."

"Don't piss on my leg and tell me it's raining, Dixie. I know you."

"She's married."

"It's so obvious now," he said. "I can practically smell her on your breath." It was pointless to keep up the ruse. I'd tell him nothing about my relationship with Pelin, but I'd stop denying it. I continued walking as he began to hoot and holler, calling me all sorts of names as his imagination ran wild: "You sonofabitch! You Mississippi leg hound!"

Judson left the following morning, still full of good cheer. We made undefined plans to get together again the next time he passed through the city on his way home. "Maybe we'll even get out the sticks and hit a few balls. See if we still got it, Dixie."

"Maybe," I said, and we embraced before he walked out the door.

Little did I know I'd never see him again. The following year, drunk, he crossed the highway median and drove his car into oncoming traffic. Whatever his faults, he was a friend of mine, the first to die.

*

Pelin arrived at my apartment, our first meeting since Judson's departure, carrying a small bag from the drugstore. I began to kiss her before she was barely through the door.

"No, my passion," she said. "You must wait."

"What's in the bag?"

"Come."

I followed her to the bathroom and watched from the doorway as she set the bag on the sink and began taking items from it: a pair of shears, a razor, and a small bottle of conditioner. "Take off your clothes," she said. She was wearing a white skirt and a green blouse but kept everything on except for her kitten heels, which she kicked off and out through the doorway into the living room.

"What are you—"

"Shh," she said, stopping the drain of the sink and filling it with warm, soapy water.

The bathroom wasn't large—just a standing shower, toilet, and sink—and after removing my clothes, I stood there feeling acutely aware of my nakedness. She lowered the lid of the toilet and set the scissors, razor, and conditioner atop it, along with a small towel she took from underneath the sink. She did not make eye contact with me or ask if I was ready. She simply grabbed the shears, knelt before me so that she was eye level with my naval, and began to trim my pubic hair. It had never been cut; I'd never considered doing so. She clipped carefully and adroitly, the bits of hair falling to the small stretch of laminate tile flooring between us.

"There is pleasure," she said, "in attending to and caring for our most intimate parts. It makes us more embodied, more aware of our sex and being. It fills us with an erotic charge at all times."

Pelin had finished trimming and ran the towel over my middle, sending wisps of human fur to the floor. The hair had been cropped from its feral state to a neat and uniform half-inch. She dipped her hands in the sink and ran them over my thighs and scrotum, as well as my penis and perineum. I took in a sharp breath of air; "excusez," she sang. The water was warm, and her hands felt good on my skin. She squirted conditioner into her hand, filling her palm, and began to cover these same parts—"Better than shaving cream"—she'd just dampened. "Don't be afraid," she said and removed the safety covering of the razor.

If she had told me what she was doing beforehand, I would have said no, worried I'd be cut, but I wasn't and, more so, I found the experience of her shaving me supremely arousing, such that I told her to stop, that I wanted her right then and there.

"No. You will stay as you are until I say so."

And she was right. I wouldn't disobey her. I'd follow her every command because if she could guide me to this state, she could also make it disappear. For a few agonizing minutes more she went on before finally pronouncing her work finished. She looked up at me from the floor.

"Okay?" I said.

"Okay."

I took Pelin by the hand, helping her up, and we kissed our way to the sink, where she turned around so that her back was facing me. She leaned forward and braced herself, clutching the counter, while I hiked up her skirt and pulled down her underwear. I entered her and thought I'd climax instantly, but I didn't. In fact, something that had never happened before was occurring: I couldn't come because I was too excited. My insides vibrated as a warm and continuous wave moved through my body. It wasn't the normal rush, rise, and release of orgasm. Some other kind of experience was happening and I watched myself have it in the mirror, the two of us breathing and grunting like the animals we were, until finally Pelin screamed out one of her murderous, dying orgasms. Afterward, I had to lie down. My insides continued to hum. I didn't know if it would ever stop. I thought I might faint. I felt terrible and wonderful at the same time. Death seemed not far away.

*

It is her eyes that I see first when I think of Pelin now. In the absence of facial affect, they took on added import. They were intensely *seeing* eyes, piercing and capable, so it felt, of the power to wilt that which fell under her regard. They were eyes from a Renaissance painting. Some years later, when I was reading a book about the Russian Revolution, I'd come across a picture of Rasputin and feel leveled. How can I convey they were her eyes, somehow transferred anachronistically back in time and placed in the sockets of that Mad Monk? I can't. No more than I can convey how beautiful and scary they were in their intensity, or the fact that those menacing eyes and their particular quality of spectation were not only the main source of her power but her allure.

*

On my way to Central Grocery, I stopped to pick up a small bouquet of tiger lilies at a flower shop. There was a crispness to my step, and I arrived before Pelin and took my spot in the queue. It was the lunch rush and the line was long but moved quickly. I ordered two of their famous muffulettas at sixteen dollars apiece, though we could have easily shared one, as most people do. It was stupid, my desire to appear, in so silly and meager a way, a man of means.

I had arrived early by intention so that I could pay for our food before she did. I'd come to feel self-conscious about the fact that Pelin paid for everything whenever the need arose. When I brought it up, she said, "You give me other things in return." She didn't mean it hurtfully—the opposite in fact—but it nonetheless monetized our time together in a way that made me uncomfortable. Our lovemaking suddenly seemed like a business transaction.

Though her face revealed nothing—could reveal nothing— Pelin was disappointed when she arrived to find me standing there, having already purchased our food and drinks. In the absence of facial expression, I'd grown the ability to discern the nuances of her moods and feelings through timbre, gesture, and intuition. Sometimes I just sensed a shift in her emotional weather the way a farmer can divine an impending storm while staring into clear blue skies.

"Why did you do that?" she said.

"I wanted to."

It was a small thing, a gesture really.

I gave her the flowers and she accepted them, finally allowing herself to nod in appreciation. I knew she loved tiger lilies, had taken note and filed it away when she'd given them to me as a housewarming gift months earlier.

"What's the occasion?" she said.

"You'll see."

There were a few tables in the back of Central Grocery, but they were already taken. It didn't matter. I preferred to walk across the street and sit on the banks of the Mississippi River, watching the water pass before me as I ate. The weather was perfect: high sixties, slight breeze, not a cloud in the sky. If you weren't from the region, it would be hard to believe it was December, that the New Year was just a couple of weeks away. We took a seat on a bench, and I removed our sandwiches from the bag and set them down between us along with our drinks. It was nice, I thought, our little picnic. Across the water from us was Algiers Point and the ferry was making its way back and forth. Beyond that were the great barges and container ships that went from port to port, traversing the globe. I wondered which belonged to Rostyk. I studied those names that I'd never before paid any attention—Hapag-Lloyd, Maersk, Hanjin, Evergreen—and I half expected to see Ozols among them.

We ate quietly, trading small talk between bites. My sandwich was tasty and I made a conscious effort to slow my pace—I tended to eat fast—while Pelin mostly picked at the olive salad and had a little of the oil-soaked bread. I thought of the sixteen dollars I'd spent on it and how at the end of the meal she'd wrap it up to throw it away without a moment's pause, not thinking of what it had cost me or that I could have taken the leftovers with me and had them for lunch the rest of the week. And when this did happen a little while later, I was too ashamed to stop her from tossing it in the garbage, too embarrassed by my relative penury in the shadow cast by her affluence.

After lunch we strolled along the Moon Walk. I'd need to head back to work soon. I wished I could take her hand but knew I couldn't. Sometimes we know the exact moment we fall in love with another person, while other times it's difficult to pinpoint one instant, understanding love to be something more fluid and subtle, the end point, seen only after the fact, at which a couple arrives after the accrual of a million smaller moments. Regardless, at that point in our history, nearly four months into our affair, though we discussed the word often but never with respect to our relationship, I was becoming aware that I was in love with Pelin.

"Well," she said, smelling her flowers, "are you going to tell me the reason for all this pageantry?"

"I submitted my applications. This morning. Before work."

She turned to me, and I could almost imagine a smile on her face. I sensed she wanted to throw her arms around me, but if she had it wouldn't have been a hug between friends but the embrace of lovers, and at the last second she remembered herself, our situation, and simply put her hand on my arm as she told me congratulations.

"I have another gift for you," I said.

"No, Dixon, I can't—"

"It cost me nothing."

Set snug against the small of my back, between my shirt and beltline was my portfolio. She'd wanted to see my photographs since the beginning, but I always put her off, saying they wasn't ready, though the truth was that I was afraid to show them to her.

"You're wrong," she said after accepting the manilla envelope from me, realizing what I'd given her. "This cost you much more than anything you could have bought, and it's much dearer to me."

"I don't know if it's good enough. What do I do if they reject me?"

"Then you keep going. You try again. You fail better." She said this as she peeked inside the envelope, inside of which were the twenty pictures I'd finally selected, and I had no idea she was paraphrasing Beckett.

Later that night after work we met at my place as usual. I had expected her to burst through the door, raring to talk about my pictures with her thoughtful insights and excitement, but she entered as normal, pausing to kiss me before continuing inside. I was disappointed. I'd half thought I might receive a call from her at work within the hour after we parted, but the afternoon hours had been deathly and slow. She thanked me again for the lunch she hadn't eaten and said, "Here's what I wanted to do when you told me you'd sent in your applications," before leaning into my chest with hers to give me a good long kiss. "Actually, here's what I wanted to do." She took my hand and led me back to the bedroom, but I was only half present and clumsy, speeding through the act in a way that couldn't have satisfied either of us. My mind was agitated, wondering why she hadn't said anything. Finally, I couldn't take it anymore and I had to ask, had she looked at my portfolio?

"No, my passion. I had appointments all afternoon. I don't want to look at them hastily. I want to give myself the time and space to appreciate and evaluate. I'm sorry, I will. I promise."

It was a Friday and we weren't able to see each other over the weekend—she and Rostyk had friends visiting for several days—and the wait was tortuous. I didn't see her until the following

Thursday, but again she didn't mention it. I couldn't bear the shame of bringing it up a second time if she still hadn't bothered to look at it. Finally, the next day, a week after I gave it to her and halfway through our normal post-work rendezvous, when our conversation had fallen into a rare tedium, she said, "Oh, I looked at your pictures. They were quite good." I waited for her to say more, but she didn't. She just sat staring at her drink. I asked what she thought. Did she see the allusions to Cartier-Bresson and Robert Frank? "Yes, of course," she said. But it wasn't derivative, was it? "No, not at all." I'd titled one of the photographs "A Simple Heart" in reference to her favorite story in the Flaubert book she had given me when we first met. Had she noticed? "Yes, that was very sweet of you," she said. This was a woman who read three books a week and could expound thoughtfully and cogently for great lengths of time on any kind of art form, and it had taken her a week to peruse at my twenty photographs and cast her banal, half-hearted verdict. *It was quite good.* She must have sensed I was disappointed or had expected more, though I tried to dissimulate my feelings, but still all she said, almost to herself this time, was, "Quite good." I imagined her on the graduate admissions committee, tossing my application into the rejection pile. I was devastated.

*

Pelin and Rostyk always travelled during the holidays to see his children from a previous marriage, so with her gone and a few extra days off from work, I found myself alone in the city. I was still smarting from Pelin's reaction to my portfolio, her doubt in me after all our early talks about whether I would become a photographer. "It's okay if I'm just a photographer and not a *great* photographer," I remember telling her in an attempt to lower the bar of expectation, though naturally I longed to be considered significant. She'd responded: "Yes, yes, yes, of course. But there is greatness and there is everything else." What a thing to say to someone who's divulged his dreams to you.

Pelin's reaction to my photos was the first real bit of tension between us, but I'd made a decision, a New Year's resolution you might say, that I would let it go. I redoubled my efforts while she was away, spending long hours walking the city with my camera. When I thought of her, I made sure it was with fondness and chastised myself when the old hurt surfaced. I missed her terribly. She was gone three weeks but would call me when she could get away. She'd given me a cell phone—an early Christmas present she said—before she left, though I hadn't asked for it and didn't want one. But I made peace with the gesture, deciding Pelin's would be the only number I called or received. When she phoned over vacation, we would exchange news and I'd tell her about what I was reading, usually a book she'd recommended. Sometimes we'd excite one another with our talk, hungry for the other's touch.

There can be pleasure in missing someone when you know you'll see them again. Still, it was a mercy when she came home. We celebrated a belated Christmas in my apartment, popping champagne she brought with her, and making love, quick and furious at first like bonobos, then slower and more tenderly each time thereafter. She presented me with a gift. Slowly I unwrapped the white wrapping paper, easing the taped edges open with my finger, to find a photograph I'd never seen before. "You're familiar with William Eggleston?" Pelin asked. I was but had not paid him much attention. Though considered the father of color photography, he was a southerner and his pictures were mostly of the region I was looking to escape; I was drawn to the city photographers I longed to be. The photograph, however, was stunning. Pelin explained that its title was "Greenwood, Mississippi, 1973," but the picture was more commonly referred to by its subject: "The Red Ceiling." The color of the red was unlike anything I'd ever seen. There was a palpable sense of violence to the picture, absent from the actual frame.

"Is this an original print?" I asked.

Pelin said nothing, which is to say she said yes.

Suddenly I was scared to touch it. I couldn't imagine what it must have cost. For weeks afterward, I would worry I'd come home from work to find the apartment ransacked, the only item worth taking gone.

"This is too much, Pelin."

"I want you to have it," she said. "Wherever you end up, your home is always your home, and someday you'll see that it's worthy of your art."

I couldn't say thank you because I couldn't speak. I just nodded and carefully set the frame down.

When it was my turn to reciprocate, there was no package for her to open. Several times she'd asked about my childhood and home life, a topic I was not eager to discuss, but I'd had an idea I thought she'd appreciate. My present to her was a proposal that we'd take a short driving tour through southern Mississippi to the town where I grew up. I would have embarrassed myself trying to buy anything for Pelin, something she could purchase herself without a second thought. I hoped the trip would deepen our intimacy and love by showing her something that would help her understand where I'd come from and account for, at least in part, what I had come to be. She loved the idea, and I could tell she was relieved I hadn't spent money on her gift. Picking a time to do the trip was trickier, but after a week or two of planning we were able to find a weekend when Rostyk was away on business and we could make our sojourn.

It was late January, a brisk Saturday in the early afternoon, when Pelin pulled onto my street in a sleek, green Jaguar sports scar. She sat at the wheel, smiling at me. She wore cat eye sunglasses and had a marigold scarf tied around her head. Proud of herself, I could see. She'd even purchased white driving gloves for the occasion—the performance and pageantry of it! Pelin was excited to drive, hadn't in a long time, she said. However, after the trauma of exiting the city—"This is madness, no?" she said as cars swam and slalomed across lanes at high speeds—and traversing the long Twin Span Bridge that carried us over Lake Pontchartrain, she pulled off onto the shoulder of Highway 10 and asked me to drive.

I obliged, and we got out and switched spots, smiling almost shyly as we passed one another at the rear bumper. Shortly after setting off again, Pelin said, "Do you smell that?" I didn't smell anything, except the leather of the car's interior. "No?" she said, taking off her driving gloves and wafting them before her face. I reiterated that I didn't. "It smells like," she said, pausing to lower her window a few inches, "ordure." The Jaguar was now filled not only with the phantom smell but also the cacophony of wind entering a car at high speed. "I think it is you," she yelled over the din.

"What?"

"The smell. I think is coming from you. From your shoes."

I prickled at her certainty that I was the source of the malodor. I said again that I didn't smell anything, that it was probably just a skunk and we'd pass through it in a minute, but she placed her hand on my arm and said firmly that she wanted me to stop the car. I did so, and once again we were on the side of the road. She inspected the bottoms of her heals and found nothing. "Now you," she said, and with a trace of annoyance I did as she asked and found a streak of mustard-colored feces across the bottom of my left shoe. I said "shit" twice, once as though identifying it and once in exasperation. Pelin bent down to gather a few small sticks nearby for me to wipe it off. Then she grabbed tissue from her purse and went to the driver's side to inspect the floor mat and tried to clean the mess I'd inadvertently made. I used spring water from one of the several bottles we'd brought along to get the rest of it off my shoe, and before long we were back on the road. The incident, a trifling thing, nonetheless discomfited me. I was embarrassed and angry with myself for being responsible and held a small animus toward Pelin because she'd known instantly that I was the agent carrying this abjection, as though it couldn't have come from her. I was being irrational and impetuous, I could see even then.

"I'm so sorry, Pelin," I said.

"It's okay, my passion. It was an accident. You didn't know."

A hint of the feculent stench remained. Once located, all I could do was smell it. I worried that I'd done permanent damage to the car, to Rostyk's car, and asked if she thought he would notice.

"It's okay. I was planning on taking it in to be fully detailed when we return anyway. He will never know."

I felt relieved but also a little hurt. She'd already planned ahead of time, prior to this incident, that she would need to remove traces of my presence from her husband's car. It made sense of course, was smart of her to have such foresight given the situation, but I couldn't help but feel a touch sad. I felt something similar when her phone rang a little while later and she answered. It was Rostyk, calling to let her know he'd made it to San Francisco safely. I could only hear Pelin's side of things, but it was easy enough to follow the flow of conversation. "Oh not much. I've got a few errands to run and then I'm having lunch with Helene later," she said in answer to the question he'd obviously asked: What are your plans today? It would have been lunacy of course for her to tell the truth, but nonetheless, in moments such as these, I became aware of the ways in which she disappeared me from her life, which had the predictable effect of making me feel disappeared, forgotten and unimportant. "I love you, too," she said and hung up.

"How's Rostyk doing?" I asked, trying to sound amiable so as to dissemble my hurt.

"Just fine," she said. "He has meetings all day, but he loves visiting San Francisco."

"Good," I said, checking my speed. "That's very good."

We were quiet for a few minutes and Pelin turned on the radio, but soon grew bored and turned it off again.

"Tell me something. Anything. A story? A joke? Whatever you like."

My comedic impulse was itself a bad joke; I was only ever funny inadvertently. But I thought a moment and recalled something one hears if you live in Mississippi long enough.

"What are the three greatest cities in Mississippi?"

She shrugged.

"Memphis, Mobile, and New Orleans."

It took her a moment, but then she did exhale a little laugh.

"Oh come on now," she said. "Mississippi can't be that bad."

She asked whether there had been a difference between southern Mississippi, where I'd grown up, and northern Mississippi, where I'd been educated.

"North Mississippi thinks everything south of Jackson is Louisiana," I said, "and south Mississippi thinks north Mississippi is what gives the state a bad name."

Again she laughed, which made me feel good.

"Tell me about your home," she said. "What was so bad about it?"

"It wasn't all bad."

"Tell me."

In sharing my portfolio with her, I'd kept one promise, and now I was finally ready to follow through on another, the one I'd made months before on that day she first brought raki over to my place and had asked me to tell her about my childhood. Given our destination, now seemed the right time. Moselle, I told her, was a small unincorporated town with no stoplights and a single post office. It was part of Jones County, and she was interested to learn about the rebellion within the rebellion that had taken place there during the Civil War, when a band of white and Black Mississippians in the area joined forces to secede from, and wage war against, the Confederacy. The Free State of Jones, they christened it, before the insurrection was defeated. An ancestor of mine was purported to have been part of the group, but to admit such a thing in Mississippi wasn't necessarily a badge of honor. Pelin had never heard the story before. "That's where you grew up?" she said, astonished. I nodded and said that that was about all Jones County had added to the annals of my country's history.

Now that the subject had been broached, I felt more forthcoming and willing to continue. I told her that my father had grown up in Moselle, as had his father and grandfather before him, and so on. As he used to say: "Our people come from that dirt." He was from a long line of farmers, though he'd shown little interest and aptitude for it himself. His education stopped after eighth grade and he bounced from job to job, doing various things. There was little work in Moselle, so he traveled to nearby Ellisville, Hattiesburg, or sometimes Laurel to find work. Odd jobs mostly. Nothing consistent.

"And your mother?" asked Pelin.

My mother had died giving birth to me, I told her, so I have no memory of her and know little of her sad, unlovely life. My father didn't like to talk about her. He'd been having an affair with another woman for years, and she moved in with us shortly after my mom was lowered into the ground. This woman, Lana, who became my first stepmother and whose apartment I was now staying in, raised me until my father met another woman named Tush, who would become my second stepmom. For a very strange and strained time both women lived in the house together until it became untenable, a fact made plain when our house was hit by a tornado. The symbolism of it was not lost on me, even as a child.

"Was anyone hurt?" asked Pelin.

"No, but the house was badly damaged, and we could no longer stay there."

"Where did you go?"

After the tornado, Lana left to start her new life in Houston, and Tush insisted we move to Hattiesburg. For all his talk denigrating Moselle and its people, my father found it hard to leave the land his family had called home for so many generations, a land that for all its faults he had risen from. But finally he gave in and we moved along with Tush's two boys from a previous marriage.

A town of fifty thousand, Hattiesburg is considered a city in a rural state like Mississippi, and I was happy to leave my hometown behind, I told Pelin. There were stores and places to eat, a university. Two of them actually. It was only fifteen miles away from where I'd grown up but a different world altogether. The move was positive for us. My father even found steady employment for the first time, managing rental properties for a wealthy landlord he nicknamed "the Kingfish." He said it with pride, not derision, happy to be employed and trusted by such a powerful and respected man. "Gotta go check on something for the Kingfish," he'd say as he rushed out the door or rose abruptly from the dinner table after a phone call. "The Kingfish needs me to come to the office."

Though I never met the man, it was through his largess, perhaps his sense of noblesse oblige, that my father had been able to afford my tennis lessons and later my private coach. Initially my interest in the sport had embarrassed him. My father always conflated my sensitivity with effeminacy and tennis only further confirmed this. He would call me Martina (after Navratilova) to get under my skin and denigrate my manhood. "Your turn to do the dishes, Martina," he might say. Or, if I was heading out to play: "Hey 'tina, did you pack your sports bra?" And if I let him get to me and got angry, he'd begin to laugh and holler: "Look out, everyone, Martina's on the rag!" I hated him, but what I hated more was that there were times I saw myself as he did. Still, I kept playing, wanting not simply to beat my opponents but dominate them, these players who were stand-ins for my father. I can't imagine he ever felt pride in my accomplishments on the court so much as the absence of shame. Enough so at least that he must have spoken of my talent at work because soon I had a coach and was able to play in bigger tournaments that eventually drew the attention of colleges. After I earned my scholarship to Ole

Miss—the first in my family to go to past high school—I wrote my father's employer a Thank You card, but to my knowledge he never saw me play a match. When I imagined him, I envisioned a large-bellied man wielding a toothpick fashioned from a raccoon penis bone, a caricature befitting the grandeur of his nickname.

Ours wasn't an affectionate household. There was no physical abuse, nothing significant anyway, but neither was there real love. Or rather, as I described it for Pelin, ours was the love of animals in a pack, as evidenced by our commitment to the group's survival. A harsh kind of affection. The closest we came to warmth was on birthdays, when Tush presented a plain sheet cake that we'd all inhale straight from the pan with our hands, no plates, no utensils. Afterward, my father would make a pronouncement, indicating the night and what little mirth it brought was over. "You are loved," he would say to whomever had turned another year older, and then we'd all go back to living as we always had. *You are loved.* That was all he was capable of. Not *I love you* or *We love you*. He could only phrase it that way, in the passive construction. You are loved.

When I said this, Pelin just sat there silently staring back at me, so I continued this excavation of my past.

During our years in Moselle, I told her, my family had been quite poor, as so many are in the area. I hated it, our poverty, and longed to escape it. Moving to Hattiesburg was an improvement, but the traces of our backwardness were still evident, would arise in certain moments that embarrassed me. For example, I knew that the way I ate, scarfing down everything as quickly as I could, stemmed from my childhood when there was uncertainty that there would be enough food for everyone, so we raced to see how quickly we could consume what was on the table. I wanted to be better than my family, because it was obvious to me that I was. I excelled at school. I cultivated interests and ambitions that were extrinsic to the means by which my family subsisted. Tennis had been one such pursuit, and I'd been fortunate to have a talent for it. My family was lucky I'd never heard of polo. I practiced hard to remove the accent from my voice and affected a mannered way of speaking that my schoolmates mocked, a comically idiotic version of the reserved, always-already-old voice I still have. I was accused of putting on airs, which I was. If I'd owned a monocle, I might have worn it. I didn't care. It was not just my family I wanted to be done with—it was all of them, everyone around me. Mississippi be damned.

I was quiet for a few moments, not sure what to say next, until a memory surfaced from oblivion. Once when I returned to Hattiesburg over summer break, I told Pelin, I struck up a conversation with a girl in a coffee shop. I'd gone there to read and suspected she was someone I might have something in common with because she too was alone, sipping her coffee, a small notebook in front of her. I was dating Sara then, but I'd developed a bad habit over the course of our relationship whereby I began intentionally putting myself in situations to be tempted by other women. I never cheated on Sara, but I would do everything to communicate my willingness and attraction to girls who interested me—flirtation, humor, an innocuous-seeming touch of their arm—but then, often when they'd reciprocated, I'd stop my pursuit cold. Despite all the emotional capital and intimacy I'd accrued by being forward and actively interested in them, I couldn't go through with it, pulled back from the ledge by the fealty of my relationship with Sara, and I'd become suddenly passive and uninterested, backing away from the potential romance I'd worked so hard to engender. I was like an alcoholic who must stare down a glass of liquor each day to test his resolve to stay sober. In any case, I continued as Pelin listened attentively, I was doing something of that with this woman, whom I found attractive, and we were carrying on quite well. She asked me about college. She couldn't afford it herself but hoped to save up for community college and maybe, one day, even to transfer to Southern Miss, Hattiesburg's state university. She wanted to know all about my experience at Ole Miss, but when I told her I was an English major, she responded, "That's cool. So you're English? What's England like?" And I was filled with such shameful disgust and a classism I hadn't the resources to support that I got up from my chair and walked out.

I'd told Pelin none of this before, and the few times I had mentioned my childhood and family I'd elided aspects of our material want. I didn't like to talk about it, some part of me still working through the humiliation and insecurity it had wrought, but it felt good to tell her now, and she listened quietly and with great interest. Mine was a very different childhood from her own in Istanbul and Switzerland, where she went to school with the children of diplomats and heirs to Middle Eastern petro-dynasties, but she expressed no shock or judgement, only sympathy and attention.

We arrived in Moselle in two hours flat. I had reached out to my stepbrother John, who was the only son of my first stepmother Lana, and who was the only family member still living in Moselle. We kept in touch sporadically, manufacturing a tenuous connection that had been absent when we were boys, when I, being eight years younger, was of little interest to him. I wrote to him, saying that I was planning on visiting Moselle with my girlfriend, and asked whether he'd like to have dinner with us. He responded that he would and insisted we stay with him. He was a preacher now and seemed to have developed an expansive generosity after finding religion.

Like good country people, we were to meet for dinner at five o'clock—Pelin gave me a sideways look when I told her—so we had a little time to kill, and we decided to explore Moselle. There was no downtown to speak of and only a handful of scattered businesses in total, so I drove her into the country, through those beautiful piney woods, to the places where I played and sought refuge as a boy. Afterward, I drove her to the spot where our house had been before the tornado made it uninhabitable. It was on a small hillock, twenty yards off a dirt road. You could still see indentions in the ground and land, but those were the only signs of the house's existence now.

Pelin and I got out of the car and approached this ghost from my childhood. "This was where the front steps were," I said, pointing to a spot a few feet in front of me. "Four of them. And they led up onto a porch, where my father and stepmother would sit in rocking chairs in the evening while us boys played in the yard." I moved forward. "This," I said, making a rectangle shape with my fingers, "was where you entered the house. There was a screen door, but the mesh had been ripped out after a fight between my parents, and my dad left the metal frame of it up, though it no longer served any purpose. I suppose it didn't matter. We kept the door open pretty much all the time anyway."

"What about the heat? What about the air conditioning?"

"What air conditioning? What heat?"

"And the flies and bugs? They just came in the house?"

I shrugged.

"You got used to it. We even named some of them."

Pelin was at my side now, holding my hand. I told her that one of my chores had been to sweep up the dead or dying palmetto bugs each morning. They were always flipped over on their back, legs sometimes slowly twitching, sometimes still, and I'd wonder how they got themselves in such a fix. "I used to grab the broom and sweep them into the dustpan, and I'd come out here on the porch and throw them over the railing." I looked over to where the edge of the porch had been, where there was nothing now. "All those years before I'd even heard the name Kafka, and there I was sweeping up little Gregor Samsas each morning."

Pelin smiled, by which I mean she nodded.

"Where was your room?" she asked.

"Our room was"—I pointed to the right, where one of the two bedrooms had been—"over here."

"Our?"

"My brothers and me."

"Four boys in one room?"

"One small room."

She made a clucking sound.

"Where were you when the tornado came?"

"Here. At home. In the bathtub."

"All six of you?"

"Seven," I said. "Lana was still living with us then."

I walked over to where the lone bathroom had been, recalling all of us huddled in and around the sallow tub as the house shook. We covered our heads, but I remember looking up once and watching through the open doorway as the portion of our roof covering the kitchen was sucked out into the heavens. Soon the tempest was gone, and we'd wander out, carefully tiptoeing through the debris to survey the damage. I went to the kitchen. It was nighttime, and I looked up at where the ceiling had been but now only saw the stars in the night sky, and for a moment it didn't strike me as strange that I could.

There were no restaurants in Moselle, so when the time came to meet John, I drove us the short distance to Ellisville, where there was an old fish camp by the watermill. We were a few minutes late, and I apologized to my brother, who stood waiting in the parking lot beside his car. John and I shook hands and I introduced him to Pelin.

"Pleasure, ma'am," he said, and with good cheer, as in an old movie, she said the pleasure was all hers.

I'd always loved the fish camp—though we rarely could afford to eat there as kids—less so for the food than for the beauty of the surrounding lake and mill. The three of us entered the restaurant and found a seat. It was half full, and my stepbrother looked around and said, "Busy. That's Saturday night for you." He'd put on a bit of weight since I'd last seen him two years prior. I knew from our correspondence that he'd been through a rough period in his twenties. He married early, like so many do around there, but he had developed a sickness for amphetamines. John became hooked and it cost him his marriage and job, but at rock bottom he'd come to Jesus and begun the difficult process of recovery. He believed, he said to us that night at the fish camp, that his life had turned for the better. "I'm washed in the blood," he said. "Ain't nothing can harm me now."

We placed our orders, fried catfish all around, and a minute later the young waitress brought back a large bowl of coleslaw and a basket of crackers. John opened a package and scooped the slaw onto a cracker before putting it in his mouth. Pelin and I followed suit. How cold and sweet it was, just as I remembered. When she got up to use the restroom, it was just my brother and me, the two of us alone together for the first time since I could remember.

"She seems nice," he said. "Real kind. Where she from?"

"New Orleans."

"No. Her family, I mean. Her origins."

I thought of Pelin's complexion and knew it stood out in a place like Moselle, where there was such a fixed and limited understanding of color. What was she? he must have thought. Too light to be Black, too olive to be native. Certainly not white.

"She's from Turkey," I said.

"Oh."

I thought by the look on his face—a different kind of blankness from Pelin's non-expression—that he didn't know where that was and started to explain, but he cut me off.

"I know Turkey," he said. "Constantinople. Ephesus. Lotta early Christianity out that way, brother."

"Right," I said, trying not to show surprise.

The dinner was heavy but tasty, and despite having washed my hands I could feel the grease still on my fingertips afterward as I gripped the steering wheel to follow John back to his place. His two-door hatchback had a busted taillight and I was self-conscious about driving Rostyk's pristine Jaguar; it felt like a clear breech of a well-defined class line. John's house was small and cozy. There was a porch with a single rusted metal rocker, once a bright aqua, and a wooden cable spool repurposed as a small table. He said he liked to sit out there in the evenings as he read the bible. We entered the house and he showed us to the room where we'd be staying. There were two twin beds lined along perpendicular walls. This was where his children, twin daughters whom I had never met, stayed when they visited. He asked if we wanted a glass of water before bed. It wasn't even seven o'clock, but he said he had to work on his sermon for the service he would lead tomorrow, which he invited us to attend. I looked at Pelin and she nodded—how could she not?—and said that sounded nice. When he left the room, we brushed our teeth and put on our pajamas before slipping into separate beds to read for a few hours until sleep was upon us and I reached to turn off the light on the bedside table.

The following morning, we readied for church. Pelin worried that she didn't have something nicer to wear. She'd been raised a secular Muslim but attended Catholic services full of pomp and ritual at the French boarding school. I told her it wasn't necessary, that this wasn't that kind of church.

"Do they speak in tongues?" she said, her voice bent with worry.

"It's not that kind of church either. You'll see."

While I'd never seen my brother preach, I knew what to expect. It would be a small country church, where there was little money and no fancy dress required. Most people wore what they did the rest of the week, not out of disrespect; it was simply what they had in their closets and dressers. It would have been strange to show up in a suit or expensive dress. My stepbrother had never been to seminary or studied formally. Pelin was surprised to learn that anyone could declare himself a preacher and start a church.

John left early after making us a hearty breakfast of eggs poached in bacon grease and his mother's cathead biscuits—how I missed those—and we showered and followed an hour later, taking our seats in a back pew shortly before the start of service. There were around twenty people sitting in two rows in a building about the size of a large living room. There was no organ, no risers for a choir. We were essentially in a large storage shed. I could feel the poor quality of the wood we walked on, warped by weather and rain soak. It lowered a half-inch wherever you stepped. The congregation was entirely white. For all the ways in which whites and Blacks lived and worked amongst each other in the South, far more so than anywhere else in the country, church was one color line that mostly held firm. My stepbrother appeared after some time, dressed in jeans and a plaid button-down shirt, his hair still wet from dragging a damp comb through it. He was jocular and engaging, a compelling speaker, something I couldn't have imagined all those years ago when we were boys and he'd steal food from my plate at dinner and wallop me with his pillow before bed.

There were a few announcements about upcoming events, a potluck and fundraiser for someone's medical bills, which was such a common thing there since many people either had terrible insurance or went without coverage. There was something sad but touching about the community coming together in this way to socialize the cost inflicted by their shared poverty. A few brief psalms followed, sung with no musical accompaniment, and then John gave his sermon on "God's awesome plan for your life," which invoked the books of Genesis, Galatians, and John, his namesake. He grew emotional and his eyes watered as he spoke about his past, attesting to the way in which the love of Jesus Christ had saved him.

"Praise be," he said, drying his eyes and composing himself for the final act of the service. "Praise be the Lord. I mean, am I a blessed man to be here with you all today, or what?" He took up a clipboard and looked out at his congregation, we who stared back at him silently. "Now who needs some prayers this week?" he asked, and immediately a dozen hands shot up. John began calling on them one by one, writing down their names and needs, building the weekly prayer list. One woman's husband's work-comp was running out and his back still wasn't better. A young man asked that his parents, whose marriage was on the rocks, be able to find their way back to each other. John wrote it all down diligently, and when the others had spoken their piece, he said he'd like to add himself to the prayer list. "I have a job interview this week," he said. "As you all know, finding steady work has been tough for me this last year. I sure could use some prayers so I can support my girls."

Pelin tugged on my sleeve and said, "He is a preacher. This is his job, no?" I whispered that he was not paid or supported in any way to do this, the way other ministers in other denominations and religions were. He did this, for this small group in his small community, as others had before him, because he believed it was needed.

The last person to raise his hand was an older man near the front. He said that he wanted to add his daughter, a pretty young woman seated beside him, to the prayer list. She was having trouble of late, periodically losing consciousness, fainting unexpectedly, and she'd been to see three doctors, none of whom knew why this was happening. Her affliction, though he didn't use the word, was idiopathic. Her name was Carol Ann. Moved once again, John spoke: "Would you all come forward and pray with me for Carol Ann." Everyone in the congregation stood and moved toward the pulpit, Pelin and myself included. Carol Ann stood next to John with her head bowed and everyone around them touched someone else, laying hands upon one another, as my brother, my stepbrother that is, said a prayer for her and all of us, some crying, some calling on the Lord, everyone saying amen. I noticed as we finished that Pelin was crying. I too was moved by the humility of this church that could disappear at any second if, say, my brother were offered a job in Alabama.

That weekend in Moselle—really it was just over twenty-four hours—was the first time that Pelin and I were able to act as though we were a couple in public. I'd told John she was my girlfriend—

she'd removed her rings—and that was how he introduced us to others after the service, friendly folks who told us to come back next week. Only in Moselle, the town where I was born, where everything was slowly dying or struggling to endure, could I hold the hand of the woman I loved, who belonged—no, was married, rather—to someone else. I felt enlivened doing so. I hugged my brother as we left the church, and, his eyes still dewy with emotion, he said, "Hang on to her, will you, knucklehead?" as he pointed at Pelin. "Don't let that idea die of loneliness." This was a reference to something my father would say: "If that boy had an idea in his head, it would die of loneliness." John was telling me not to be stupid, not to let her get away from me. Then he hugged me again, and Pelin as well, and we got in our car and drove back to New Orleans. Rostyk would arrive home Tuesday morning, but there was still time for Pelin to have the car cleaned.

*

One night we were sitting on the porch of a yellow cottage in the Bywater. It was a restaurant called The Country Club and out back on its patio was a clothing-optional pool. I'd heard about it from someone at work and suggested to Pelin that we go there for dinner—I didn't mention the pool—since it was close to my apartment and far away from Pelin's neighborhood. She liked the sound of it, so we went and had dinner, sitting on the porch of the beautiful old house. As we ate our meal, I told her about the pool. I knew she'd find it amusing, but to my surprise, seized by whim, she suggested we give it a try. When I said we didn't have suits, she shrugged and said: "We will go nude."

After dinner we walked through the house out back to the patio, where we paid a small fee and were given towels. There were separate changing rooms for men and women. Inside were lockers and a sauna, in which lounged several naked men. One was going down on another and the third gentleman just sat there, a few feet away, and leaned his head back against the wall, perspiring, as if nothing at all were happening beside him. I took off my clothes and walked outside with nothing but my wallet.

There were probably fifteen people, either standing around, swimming in the pool, or sitting in the hot tub, and there were twice as many men as women. I went to the outdoor bar and ordered drinks, and when I turned around, I found that Pelin was already in the pool, treading water, her long black hair tied up so as not to get wet. I set my wallet on a nearby deck chair and got into the pool, handing her the drink. She wrapped her legs around me and we kissed under the starlight that shimmered and refracted off the water's surface. A little while later we got another round of drinks, gin and tonics that came in big plastic cups, and we made our way to the hot tub. There was a Black woman with dreadlocks sitting across from us, her breasts floating, it seemed, on the bubbles shooting from the jets below. She saw me staring at her and said, "Wanna suck on my titty? It'll put hair on your lip." Then she laughed and kissed the girl next to her, a young white woman.

Soon a man got into the tub beside Pelin and started talking to us. Rather, he was talking to her, and I felt myself getting a little jealous. I put my arm around Pelin to indicate we were together. A little while later, he said he was leaving, followed by: "Would you like to come home with me?"

"She's with me," I said.

"The invitation was to both of you." He got out of the hot tub and stood above us, dripping in the moonlight, unbothered by his nakedness. "The three of us can have a good time together," he said, turning his gaze to me. "I saw you staring at me earlier, just as you are now."

I looked away, shaking my head. I tried to laugh, but it was swallowed by a sudden inaudible fury. He stood waiting for an answer, but I couldn't speak.

"Thank you for the invitation," said Pelin, "but we have other plans."

He said nothing, just rolled his eyes and walked away, frustrated to be rebuffed. I felt Pelin's hand squeeze my thigh gently a few times in a kind of lovers' Morse code: I'm here, It's okay, I love you.

A few days later, when our night at The Country Club was receding from memory, Pelin said, almost out of nowhere, "Maybe it could have been fun."

It was after work and we were at my place, as usual. We'd just made love in a position I'd never tried and afterward we laughed, holy-shit eye-rolling at the wonder of it. But now we were coming down from the high, our breathing starting to calm. That's when she'd said it, maybe it could have been fun.

"What do you mean?" I said. "You didn't enjoy that?"

"No, no, no," she said. "I loved it. Trying new things is exciting." I could see she was drowsy with recollect, her mind elsewhere now after we'd been so focused and present with each other only a minute earlier. "The young man who invited us home with him. At the pool. Maybe it could have been fun."

"You wanted to go?"

I felt the prickle of jealousy.

"Only if you came with."

It was impossible for me to imagine doing so, not knowing what would be expected of me in such a scenario, not wanting to share her with anyone. My mind simply couldn't go there. And yet, so many times she had forced me out of my comfort zone—intellectually, sexually, and otherwise—to my benefit that to respond the way I felt, the way the culture had taught me to—*I don't go in for gay shit*— would have exposed not just intolerance but cowardice and a lack of sophistication, of cultivation. So I aped a blasé broadmindedness I didn't feel. "I think you're right," I said, only able to parrot her own words back to her: "Maybe it could have been fun."

*

Carnival had begun, as it always does, on Twelfth Night, January sixth. That year Mardi Gras fell late in February, and when it arrived I was already sick of parade season, with the city carved up and cordoned off by police barricades demarking routes. It was virtually impossible to get anywhere. About the only things I cared to see were the Mardi Gras Indians, though I was never able to find them, and the raucous and vulgar Krewe du Vieux, which I did. It was hard to miss since the parade started a few blocks from where I lived. The theme that year was "2001: A Space Fallacy," though it should have been spelled "phallusy" for all the bawdy decorations and costumes. I'd brought my camera to document it all, and I still have the picture I took of a float satirizing Bill Clinton's travails— George W. Bush was president then, having been sworn into office just seven days before Mardi Gras, but the country couldn't get enough of Slick Willy—holding his massive erection before a kneeling Monica Lewinsky. I also took one of Bush, snorting cocaine off an empty bottle of Jack Daniels, but I've somehow lost it over the years.

When I showed the pictures to Pelin at my apartment one evening after work, she asked about my politics, a subject we'd never really broached. She was studying one image my camera had captured of a float dedicated to the Florida recount and the Supreme Court decision that gave the recent election to Bush. I told her I paid politics little attention, that it didn't interest me. "I guess I'm sort of agnostic when it comes to that."

"You are not an agnostic."

"No? What am I?"

"You're an aesthete. Like me," she said. "Art and beauty. That is our politics."

It was a position that could only have been staked from the safety of privilege, but I couldn't—or didn't want to—see that then.

Many businesses shut down for the culmination of the season, and I was pleased not to go to work the morning of Lundi Gras. Pelin and I didn't go to see King Zulu arrive via boat to meet King Rex, the ritual that initiates the start of Mardi Gras. Instead, we ignored the city and its tireless pursuit of public, conspicuous revelry and holed up in my apartment to celebrate privately. Despite the limitations posed by the kitchen's inadequate setup, to say nothing of my limitations as a chef, I decided I would cook for her. There was one dish I'd come to enjoy, and I set about making it. The stove didn't work, so I boiled a large pot of water on the hot plate and added spaghetti and salt and oil and let it cook until I threw a strand at the wall and it stuck. Then I drained it and set the pasta aside in a bowl with a tablespoon of butter while I cooked the sauce in a smaller pot on the hot plate. Pelin watched it all, amused, as I raced around the small kitchen in my apron, bumping into things, trying to do three tasks at once. I must have looked like Jack Lemmon in *The Apartment*, overwhelmed, using the strings of his tennis racket as a colander. I set the table and dressed the arugula-and-spinach salad, opened a bottle of red wine I'd purchased, one I knew Pelin liked. I took out a cutting board to slice the baguette, but Pelin stopped me. "In France," she said, taking the bread from the board, "they just do this," and tore off a hunk. I grated fresh Pecorino over our pasta, not the cheap heavily processed parmesan my family called "snow cheese" that we used to crop-dust over everything.

We sat down to dine, clinked glasses as we made eye contact and told one another, in so many Turkish words, that we had sex with each other's mother, a joke that never stopped amusing us. Then we ate and when we were finished, as a digestif, I poured calvados into the smart cordial glasses Pelin had recently bought for me. I brought over a plate of pralines I'd picked up at Aunt Sally's to nibble on.

"Dessert," I said.

"Lagniappe," she replied and moved to kiss me.

We were in bed making love when there was a knock at the door. The only person who ever did so was lying beneath me, and I filled with panic as we scrambled to dress. Rostyk, I thought. He'd found out. There was a second knock and a few seconds later, as I was pulling a shirt over my head, the door swung open. Standing there was not Rostyk but my first stepmother, Lana, keys in hand.

"What are you doing here?" I said, closing the bedroom door so Pelin would have a little privacy, though it was no use hiding. Lana had seen us.

"I emailed that I was coming for Carnival," she said.

Damn it, I thought. I hadn't checked my account since Judson's visit. It wasn't intentional. At that point it was possible to live without the internet, and, not having easy access to it, I often forgot it existed.

"Oh," I said. "Of course."

"I tried calling, too, but you must have been at work." She looked over at the phone on the wall. "Guess I should get an answering machine for it, huh?"

"No, that's okay, come on in," I said, suddenly anxious to make her feel welcome, remembering after all that it was she who had let me stay there free of charge the last two years. "We were just, uh," I said, turning back to the bedroom, where Pelin had just stepped out, fully dressed.

"Caught you rolling around in the hay, didn't I," Lana said. "Shoot, I'm sorry as hell."

I shook off her apology and moved to hug her before introducing Pelin.

"My son," Lana said, then stopped as she looked at me, and began again. "My other son, John, said he enjoyed meeting you very much."

"He was so kind to us," Pelin said, "and an inspiring preacher. We had a wonderful visit to Moselle."

"He's doing okay, sure enough. Finally finding his way out of the desert."

What followed were a few awkward minutes of forced invitations and proposals that the three of us do something together when it was obvious that what we all wanted—what we all needed—was for Pelin to go, which she did, inventing an excuse about meeting a friend for a Lundi Gras event. We watched Pelin leave, and after the door shut, Lana turned to me: "Got anything to drink?"

When I was young, after my father had taken up with Tush, Lana and I formed a closeness that had not existed prior to him leaving her. For a time, it was an alliance against him, in opposition to him, and though it faded some over the years, we at least remained, if not close, then much closer than we'd been in the years we'd lived under the same roof, and so we continued to be all these years later, after the wounds my father inflicted on us had begun to heal.

"Darl," she said, referring to my father, "was a hard dog to keep on the porch. Never could bring him to heel. He'd run after any bottle-blonde with a pair of store-bought titties, wedding ring or not. I didn't think you'd be the same way."

She didn't say this unkindly or with judgment. I didn't know how to respond.

"John told me she was your girlfriend, Dixie."

I hated being called that, but it would have been far stranger to hear a family member call me Dixon.

"She is," I said.

"Then whose ring's she wearing? You suddenly come into money I don't know about?"

"I love her."

"She's married."

I nodded.

There I was, the other man, the secret lover, the third party threatening Rostyk's marriage, the way Tush had Lana's, and the way Lana herself had my poor dead mother's.

"That's hard," she said. "I don't envy you. I remember that, the lying. The guilt."

"I doubt my father ever felt guilty."

"Does Pelin? Do you?"

"Of course," I said instinctively, but the truth was more complicated than that.

In the early days of our affair, Pelin and I were too in lust to feel the full weight of guilt. Of course, I didn't have to go home to Rostyk every night. Pelin, for her part, dealt with it the way we mostly do difficult things: by not dwelling on it. Or so it seemed to me. She rarely talked about it, but when she did, she was able to frame it in the least damning manner. I recall her once saying early on that though Rostyk would certainly not approve of our relationship, he must on some level be grateful to me because of how happy I made her, and that joy also enhanced their own life together. But now it was different. All these months later, we were beyond lust. We were firmly in love with one another, and the light on our transgression had dimmed because we were so habituated to the situation. What was once illicit now simply felt like the way we lived, part of the new norm we'd established. If I'd been able to understand and articulate that to Lana then, what I would have said in answer to her question was that the guilt I sometimes felt wasn't for the affair. The guilt I sometimes felt was that I no longer felt guilty for the affair.

"Well," my stepmother asked, "what will you do?"

I answered her honestly.

I said, "I don't know."

*

On the day Rostyk would tell Pelin he knew about the affair, she and I had met at NOMA and walked through the museum together. It was the weekend and many were out admiring the art. Going there with Pelin was an inversion of the experience I had bringing Judson there months prior. Then I'd had the intellectual upper hand and I remarked on all the paintings and sculptures, manufacturing an authority that was utterly fallacious. But going with Pelin now, I was the one who followed and listened. And yet, I was, by then, also trying to assert myself as someone who did more than just take notes. I remember stopping before a painting of Medusa, the familiar image of the woman, a Gorgon with snakes for hair, turning a man to stone with the repulsiveness of her face. We were looking at it and I said that I thought of the Medusa story as a metaphor for the twin male impulses toward the female sex: desire and revulsion. I said this confidently, as if it were my own insight, when it was actually something I once heard a professor say in class. Pelin looked at the painting and thought a moment.

"No," she said. "You're overcomplicating it. It's a simple story, perhaps the oldest. Men and women forever drawn to one another, forever destined to suffer because of it."

Actually, I can't remember whether this conversation took place on the day Rostyk found out about us—it was probably a few days earlier, possibly a week or more—but it would be fitting if it had. He'd grown suspicious because their physical intimacy, which was already infrequent, had become nonexistent, so he hired someone to follow her and the investigator had pictures of her entering and exiting my apartment at the same time several days running. I could imagine Rostyk and the PI meeting to discuss his findings because I'd already watched the scene unfold in a dozen films. The terrible cliché of it all.

I didn't find out about any of this until Pelin showed up at my apartment after work without her usual ebullience. This was early March, when the crawfish boils had begun, and you'd see their red shells littering the streets and smell the Cajun seasoning coming off the boiling vats blocks away, the surest sign in the Gulf Coast that spring had arrived. I could smell it when I opened the door to let her in. Pelin kissed me, hugging me a beat longer than usual, before coming inside. I knew something was different and asked if she was okay. She didn't answer, just requested that I make us each a raki, so I did. Trying not to spill liquid over the lip of the glasses, I brought them to the couch, where she sat smoothing the seam of her white dress. We clinked glasses from the bottom, and

I said "anani sikerim" but for once she didn't. We were quiet a few moments, and without her saying so I suddenly understood.

"Rostyk knows," I said.

She nodded, not in the manner I'd grown accustomed to that meant she was happy, smiling in her own way. This was a different nod, smaller, slower, saddened, meaning simply: yes.

"How?"

I listened to her explain what happened and afterward I sat there, silent. I thought about how when this began, our affair, it had seemed temporary, at least insofar as I had plans and desires to leave New Orleans and go to graduate school. So far, however, I had received three rejection letters, had been waitlisted at another school, and I was coming to see it as unlikely that I would be accepted anywhere. While it was disappointing, the thought of staying in New Orleans for another year with Pelin had become increasingly attractive. I couldn't see a way in which she would ever willingly extricate herself from her marriage, but I could see a way in which we could carry on as we had all these months, as secret lovers. I'd even tried to convince myself that the arrangement suited me, that I was getting the best of two competing worlds I so desired: one a world of passionate intimacy and the other of thoughtful solitude. I had the love of an intelligent and beautiful woman but also the time and space to make pictures. That it also gutted me when she left my apartment each day, or when I imagined her sleeping in bed next to Rostyk, or when I couldn't see her because she was out at an engagement with him, or a dozen other small ways in which the situation wounded me—those I tried to downplay, if not repress entirely. But all of this, the possibilities and limitations of our situation, had been predicated on one basic fact: Rostyk not knowing.

"What happened?" I asked finally. "After he told you."

"I didn't deny it," she said. "He was furious to play the cuckold of course."

"He didn't...strike you, did he?"

"Are you kidding? Rostyk? Never. He threw a two-thousand-dollar bottle of Scotch at the wall."

She told me he yelled at her for a long time but that when it had exhausted him, his anger, they were able to talk calmly. They spoke through the night. He wanted to know details, who I was and how we'd come to be lovers.

"Don't worry," she said. "He's not one to show up on your doorstep with a baseball bat."

"Yeah, but he could hire someone else to do it for him."

I hadn't intended the remark to be funny, but Pelin laughed because, I suppose, she knew he would never do such a thing.

Rostyk did not throw her out of the house or threaten divorce. He loved Pelin, he told her. He wanted them to stay together and was willing to overlook this transgression. She spoke in his voice: "'Of course, this is all dependent on whether you stop seeing this other person, this boy.'" She waved her hands with disgust as she said this, acting out Rostyk's part.

"What did you say?"

"I told him I would."

"And yet here you are."

"I said I needed to see you one last time, to explain."

"I understand."

Despite the shock of these revelations, I felt a strange sense of equanimity. She'd explained what had happened and what would need to happen for her life, as she knew it, to remain undestroyed. My feelings didn't seem to factor into the equation. I wasn't going to get on my knees and beg and I certainly wasn't going to fall to pieces, at least not in front of her. There was so little I could offer her to offset all that Rostyk did.

"I must go," she said and set down her drink.

"Wait. This is it?"

"I'm sorry."

"I *love* you, Pelin."

She looked at me a few moments and then kissed me.

"I love you too, my passion, but I…"

I could see she had prepared for this conversation well in advance, which accounted for her dispassionate delivery and resolve, but it was only here, in what were to be our final moments, that I could see her struggle, unable to say what she needed to say so that she could leave my apartment and return to her other life. I didn't feel angry and what I felt wasn't yet hurt. What I felt then was sympathy.

"I know, Pelin. I understand," I said, and I took her hand, accompanied her to the door, and opened it, watching her walk down the stairway as she dug through her purse, looking for a tissue. I went back inside and sat on the couch, unsure what to do with myself. An image came to mind, a picture I'd seen with her at the museum. Not the Medusa painting. This one had looked like a pile of discarded clothing, what I had thought initially were intimates and underthings strewn on the floor, as if by lovers. But when I got close to it and read the wall label, I realized that it wasn't clothing at all. They were the discarded parts of a slaughtered lamb, the offal.

*

In the days that followed, I moved through the world like a somnambulant. Everything felt both familiar and strange. In this unheimlich state, I urinated in the sink at work instead of washing my hands and thought nothing of it. The next day, I placed my peanut butter sandwich in the pot of a nearby plant when I noticed it needed water, and it didn't seem odd until later when I asked myself whether it had really happened or was it a revenant from my unconscious life in dreams. I thought of Pelin incessantly, without reprieve. I returned home from work each day and watched the clock tick toward the time when I'd normally hear her knock on my door and I'd feel shattered when it didn't come. I went to bed and ran my hands and nose over the sheets, trying to find any trace of her scent. I tried reading in the cloffice, but even that space, so long a sanctuary, left me unable to still my mind. The apartment itself, this room that had contained almost the entirety of our relationship, and thus was a symbol of it, came to feel intolerable, and so I began taking long walks all over the city. I'd bring my camera but found myself unable to take a single picture.

One evening I set out from my apartment and walked all the way uptown until I got to Audubon Park. When I returned home, I was surprised to find five hours had passed. I thought I'd been gone an hour or so. I exhausted myself with these nightly ambles, I had to, so that I could climb into bed and not think.

I tried doing the same thing the following night—wearying myself into oblivion—but after reaching Audubon Park and turning around to make my way home, I stopped when I arrived in the Garden District. I wandered down Magazine slowly, feeling unseen, like the haints my father used to swear roamed the piney woods around our house, past the bars and boutiques, looking at the people doing what people do in those kinds of establishments. I'd grown accustomed to avoiding this part of town, but now here I was. I veered off onto side streets and made my way into the Lower Garden District. I knew where Pelin's house was, but I'd never seen it until that night when I was standing before it in the failing light. It was the sort of grand home one envisioned when thinking of New Orleans: Greek-Italianate revival, ionic columns, rod iron fencing, magnolia trees—the whole shebang. I stood on the sidewalk taking in the great manse, snapping photographs of it, hoping to catch sight of Pelin passing by a window, waiting for the green Jaguar to find its way home, which after some time—I can't say how long—it did. The car crept along the street until it found a spot a few feet away from me, nestling up to the curb with an ease and familiarity. For a few moments the Jaguar continued to run, and I stared into the tinted windows, unable to make out anything. Then the engine cut, the driver's side door opened, and Rostyk got out.

He was dressed in dark trousers and a light fitted shirt. He had a salted beard and silver hair styled back, wavy with product. He was in the early stages of becoming portly, looking like a man given to gustatory indulgence and unrepentant for it. His resting face carried a trace of self-satisfaction or judgment; it was the face of one whose smile is hard won.

"Mr. Ozols," I said.

"Yes." We were silent a moment. "Go on."

"I'm…"

He squinted at me, then at the camera hanging round my neck, and his eyes relaxed.

"It's you," he said. "My wife's—"

"Yes."

"Jums ir dazas pauti."

"I don't know what that means."

"Then you should learn Latvian." He smiled briefly and then it was gone. "What is it you want?"

"I'm in love with your wife," I said.

"What do you expect me to do with this information?"

"Can I speak to her?"

He had been so casual, so unsurprised, by my appearance that I thought perhaps he'd had his man tailing me, feeding him information about my whereabouts and movements. Then suddenly his equanimity vanished and he took a step toward me, as though he were going to strike me but stopped and turned away, waving an arm toward the Jaguar.

"Get in the car," he said.

"Why?"

He didn't answer. We stood staring at one another, his arm still pointing toward the door, until I got in, and soon we were off. I began to ask where we were going, but he cut me off with a slow shhhhhhhhh. He drove slowly, deliberately, snaking through the streets of the neighborhood. Bright lights—streetlamps, stoplights, headlights, signage from bars and restaurants—appeared and disappeared in the darkness around us. I heard Rostyk burp, small and unintentional, almost inaudible. I glanced side-eyed at him, but he looked straight ahead at the road, his lips open just enough to reveal an overbite. The camera sat heavy in my lap. I imagined taking a picture of him but didn't dare. I recalled the only other time I'd been in this car, when I drove Pelin to Moselle, and remembered the awful smell I'd inadvertently brought into it on my shoe. I wanted to tell him that I'd desecrated his prized automobile when finally he spoke.

"Do you know the history of this district?" Not waiting for me to answer, he continued: "The entire land that makes up this neighborhood was once owned by a single family. The Livaudais Plantation. In the 1840s it was purchased by businessmen who broke it up and sold it off in parcels. They thought of it as the American answer to the French Quarter. Even as more people moved here the homes had a lot of land, which meant they could have gardens. That's how it became known as the Garden District." Rostyk reached his hand across my chest to point out the window. "Beautiful old mansions now, but once upon a time the only homes here aside from the master's house were slave shacks." He turned to meet my eyes. "Do you think you could ever give her something like this? Do you think Pelin would ever lower herself to see you as an equal?"

"She loves me."

"She fucks you. Youth tends to conflate the two."

"I love her."

"That's your problem now. What you had is over."

I couldn't disagree. Pelin had told me as much herself the last time I'd seen her. Rostyk continued driving until we were parked on the street in front of my apartment. He tipped his head toward it as if to say, "This you?" But of course he knew it was.

"You were taking pictures of my house," he said. "When I arrived. Why?"

"I don't know," I said. "Sometimes I'm moved to take a photograph and it's pure instinct."

"Yes, but this wasn't instinct. You knew what you were doing." He paused. "Can I see it, your camera."

"No."

"Give it to me."

I clutched it tightly. Pelin had laughed about Rostyk's capacity for violence, but I felt something dark and menacing come between us in the car. I understood that in coming there and confronting him I'd channeled a kind of bravery not too far removed from insanity. It was the courage of a kamikaze pilot. I felt fear but also the invigoration that comes with having stared down my own annihilation.

I handed him my camera and he turned it so that it was pointed at himself, staring at the lens as if he might take a self-portrait. "Hmm," he said, bouncing it in his hands a little like a baby. "Heavier than I would have thought." Then, suddenly, he got out of the car, raised the camera over his head, and slammed it onto the street, where it shattered, the pieces flying every which way. "But still easily broken." I was shocked into stillness, silence. Rostyk looked at the scattered remnants of my Nikon CP850, then removed his billfold and counted out ten one-hundred-dollar bills. Calmly he got back into the car and handed the money to me. "Find yourself a new camera and a new girlfriend," he said. "Now get out of my car." When I didn't move, his tone sharpened. "I said get out." I unbuckled my seatbelt and opened the door, looking back at him one last time. "Go!"

The following evening, I came home from work to find Pelin waiting outside the stairwell that led up to my apartment.

"What were you thinking?" she said. "Coming to my home like that? Confronting Rostyk?"

"I was brave for you," I said. "I will always be."

Unlike the last time I saw her, Pelin's composure crumbled from the start. She was not an actress blocking a well-rehearsed scene; she was speaking spastically, chastising me one moment, saying she missed me the next. How strange to hear someone say these things, and in such a manner, while maintaining a countenance unperturbed by emotion. We began to kiss, and then I was leading her up the stairway and into the apartment, and then we were in bed making love again.

*

How easily we fell back into it. We assumed our old ways of being, though our relationship had changed. We began to look forward, outward, to imagine a life together not just as lovers but partners. For the first time we spoke about a future, one that we cohabitated together. After my encounter with Rostyk, Pelin informed him that she wanted a divorce and had moved in with a friend for the time being. I couldn't believe she was leaving him for me. When I said that one day, she said, "I'm leaving him for me, not you, my passion. I need this. You are not beholden to me." The thing was, I wanted to be. Suddenly escaping to cities of the east or west coast felt less appealing. I floated the idea of going to graduate school at Tulane or UNO. We said—"I love you"—often to one another, every other sentence it seemed, as though it were a prayer uttered to protect us from forces outside our control. But that was the thing: we had complete control of the situation. We could choose to be together if we wanted. The prospect terrified and thrilled us at once.

In the rush of our second chapter together, Pelin had begun sending me love letters, which I cherished. They were a more concentrated form of her extemporaneous thought and speech, which is to say they were incredibly intelligent and eloquent, something I was impressed by and a little jealous of, given English was probably her third or fourth language. I suggested she try her hand at writing seriously, novels or essays perhaps. She clearly had a gift, but she scoffed at the suggestion.

One day in early April I went to the mailbox hoping to find one of her letters when what I found instead, buried behind a few pieces of junk mail, was a letter from Columbia informing me that I had been accepted off the waitlist into their MFA program. I'd been rejected from all the other schools and, given how competitive it was, I'd given up hope of getting in off the waitlist. But here it was, a letter telling me otherwise. I didn't feel excited because it didn't yet feel real. It was as though I'd experienced a temporary emotional aphasia; I didn't know what I felt about this unexpected news. I tried to imagine New York City, but even the stock images of towering skyscrapers and yellow taxis braying in crowded streets escaped me. It may as well have been Micronesia.

I debated whether to say anything to Pelin. I could throw the letter away and keep on living as I had, as we had, as if I'd never been offered this opportunity. Our reunion over the past twelve days had turned us into addicts who think the high will last forever, even if they know it can't. I can see it now for what it was, the desperate manic madness of a love affair approaching its death rattle, but we clung to it as we did to one another, tightly, until the blood was wrung from our knuckle-white hands.

When she arrived at my apartment later that day, she held a box of Turkish Delights in one hand and her purse in the other. I was still trying to find my words and simply pointed at the envelope on the kitchen counter. "What's wrong?" she said. Again, I pointed at it, and she walked over and set down the box of candies so she could pick up the letter. "What's this? Is it from Rostyk? I told him if he threatened you, I'd get a restraining order."

"Read it," I said, and she did.

"Oh," she said a few seconds later. Perhaps she'd forgotten about it, or, like me, assumed I wouldn't get in, and she just stood there holding the letter until she remembered that this was, supposedly anyway, great news. "You got in," she said, nodding, and then she moved to embrace me. "Congratulations, Dixon." It was so rare to hear her say my name and it felt oddly formal compared to the usual endearment by which she addressed me. We were already distancing from one another, seconds after the revelation.

"I can't believe it," I said.

"Aren't you happy? This was your dream."

"I don't know."

We were quiet a few moments, processing, and then she spoke: "I knew you'd get in." I could tell by the way she said this, sadly, that she was earnest, not simply saying what she thought she should. "When I saw your portfolio."

"I was under the impression you didn't care for my pictures," I said, recalling how much it had hurt me, her indifferent response. *It was quite good.* "That's why I never showed you anything else."

"Your photographs were excellent. That's why I never asked to see any more of your pictures."

"Why?"

"Because I knew you'd get in and that you'd leave."

"I don't have to leave."

"Yes, you do. We both know it. You don't turn this down. You must go to New York."

The following day, her final love letter arrived. Of course, she'd written it before we learned of my acceptance. She said how much she loved me and described so compellingly what our life together would look like, an imagined life that no longer seemed possible. I felt the temporal chasm of that moment devouring me: me with the knowledge of the present trying to connect to an unknowing Pelin of the recent past, of only a day or two earlier. I read it over and over as I ate the entire box of Turkish Delights, stuffing myself until I had to lie down on the bathroom floor, clutching my stomach. I don't even like sweets.

*

That Saturday evening I arrived at Hotel Monteleone, walking through the lobby past the front desk and spinning Carousel Bar to the elevator bank, where I waited a few moments before boarding

and punching the button for the third floor, as I'd been instructed
to. I was wearing my lone suit and removed the invitation from the
coat pocket. Blue lettering embossed on thick white card stock:

You are invited to a party in celebration of Dixon Still's
acceptance to Columbia University
Saturday April 7, 6pm
Hotel Monteleone, Room 318
Dress: Cocktail attire / Naked
Bisou,
P

I had worried that showing her the acceptance letter would
distance us, and for a short while it did. She said she needed a
little time to process it, which was understandable—I did too—and
we didn't see each other for several days. I was beginning to think
that whatever we'd had was over when, unexpectedly, this invitation
arrived in my mailbox and with it the familiarities of our love. There
was the sense that we could celebrate my impending departure as
lovers should, choosing to savor the sweet over the bitter.

I exited the elevator, momentarily discombobulated as I studied
the signs to see which direction room 318 was located. When I
knocked on the door, Pelin's familiar voice called out for me to enter,
and slowly I eased it open. She was sitting in a blue-upholstered
Bergere chair by a small wooden table, upon which rested a bottle
of Veuve Clicquot Brut, chilling in ice, and two glasses. I stepped
into the room, taking it in. It was grand and beautiful, the effect
I knew Pelin intended it to have. A brass chandelier threw soft
light on alternating gold-and-cream patterned wallpaper. A large
mahogany bureau hid the television that would have ruined the
romance of it all if left out in the open. The king-size bed seemed
large enough to swim laps in. The thick outer drapes of a large
window overlooking the Quarter were open, but the thin inner
lining was closed, giving the whole tableau the gauzy-gossamer feel
of a dream.

Pelin nodded at me; I smiled back at her.

"It's beautiful," I said, and then she stood. She was wearing a
fetching white dress. "*You're* beautiful," I said as we embraced.

"You recognize?" she asked, meaning the dress.

I thought a moment.

"The day we met," I said. "Faulkner House."

"And this," she said, pulling at the lapels of my charcoal suit, "I recognize from the ballet."

"I'll always remember that night."

There we were, repurposing earlier moments of our relationship in a new setting. We were in a present manufactured from a known past and speculative future. I began to kiss her, wanting to usher her to the bed, but she stilled me. "First champagne," she said, "We must celebrate your accomplishment." She motioned to the table—"Would you open?"—and I walked over and took the bottle from its ice bath, removed the foil, twisted the wire, and popped the cork. As the foam ran over my hand, I poured a little into the glasses. Each drop set off a small explosion of fizzing cascades that when settled left only a small amount of wine in the bottom of each flute, as if self-evaporated by pageantry. We said our usual toast and sipped. "Congratulations, Dixon," she said. "I'm happy for you, even if I'm sad for me."

"Pelin, I—"

"No, my passion, please. I've cried enough the last few days. I want this to be happy. I want to enjoy the rest of our time together."

"And then what?"

"And then you go to New York and I have my life here."

"Will you go back to Rostyk?"

"No. I left him. For me, remember."

"And us?"

"We become a memory," she said. "A happy one. As vivid in my mind as one of your photographs."

Though I was able to resist the urge, I felt a young man's desire to protest, to make grand gestures and declarations of eternal love, but I knew she was right. I had no words, so I used my mouth to sip more champagne and then to kiss her. I felt the familiar waves of desire course through me and set my glass down so I could run both hands over her as we embraced. I started to lift up the hem of her dress when she pulled away.

"I have a gift for you," she said.

She urged me over to the bed and I went, pausing to take off my shoes and suit jacket before lying down on the great expanse of the white comforter. I began unbuttoning my shirt as I watched her, standing at the foot of the bed, waiting for her to remove her dress and join me.

"We're ready," she called out over her left shoulder.

At her command, the closed door of the bathroom opened and there stood a man, naked but for a pair of black trunks. He was short and muscular with a thin waist and thick torso that gave him a cartoony appearance, a human Mighty Mouse. For a moment it seemed this stranger was a neighboring guest who'd inadvertently stumbled into the wrong room.

"Can we help you?" I asked.

"No," the man said. "But I think I can help you."

"What's going on?"

I looked to Pelin. She was nodding.

"He is your gift."

"A gift? What do you mean *gift?*"

"I thought it might be fun."

"What might be fun?"

"For the three of us to..."

I looked at him and then back at her.

"Why the fuck would you think that?"

"I thought you said he—" the man started to say, but Pelin motioned him away with the wave of a hand and he disappeared behind the bathroom door again.

I rolled over to the side of the bed as Pelin moved toward me. I could feel my body flooding, not with the warmth of desire but the heat of ungranted exposure, of shame and defensiveness and anger.

"I'm sorry, my passion. I wanted to do something special for you."

"By inviting another man into our bed?"

"I thought you were open to this."

"Why?"

"We talked about it. After the night at the pool. The young man who invited us home. Remember?"

I hadn't forgotten the conversation so much as it hadn't felt real because I hadn't been honest.

"You said—"

"Am I not enough for you? You want him, too?"

"No," she said, "I thought you might want to have both of us, my passion."

"What?"

She repeated herself.

"What makes you think I want to be with a man?"

"I just thought—"

"What is it about me that makes you think I want to fuck another man?"

In that moment I felt the weight of my father saying tennis was a women's sport, calling me Martina. I felt Judson expecting me to come out to him the day I told him I was quitting the team, and the man on the street calling me Judson's bitch-boy. I felt the young man at the pool inviting us back to his place. What had I done to give people the impression I was something I was not? That's what I was thinking, but the response I was having was rooted in a different question I hadn't yet learned to ask: How had other people come to know me better than I knew myself? Pelin was speaking, but I couldn't engage. My brain closed off a certain portion of itself. I could not discuss the thing she wanted to discuss. I was putting on my shoes. I was buttoning my shirt. I was stepping out of her grasp and making my way to the door. I heard her voice and saw her mouth moving, but I was the one with a blank, impassive face now. It was as though she were speaking in her native tongue and I was unable to understand or respond until I was turning the handle to leave and she set her palm against the door to stop me. That's when I found language again. That's when I was able to say the things that would allow me to exit the room.

"You can have him to yourself," I said.

"I don't want him, my passion. I'll send him away. I want only you. I'm sorry."

"You've had your fun. You've embarrassed me. Now leave me be."

"Dixon."

"Leave me alone, you old cunt."

I could hear him speaking through me. My father. I'd become a vessel for him.

Pelin said nothing. Finally I made eye contact, saw the confusion and hurt in her eyes, then her hand fell from the door so I opened it and was gone.

*

Though I'd not leave New Orleans for almost two months, that evening in the hotel was really the end. I'd revealed a part of myself neither of us had ever seen or were prepared for and it broke us. No matter how much or how earnestly I apologized—which I'd started doing the following day once I'd calmed down and thought things through—we could never find our way back to one another, at least not in any way that resembled the love we'd known. She accepted my apology and even apologized herself for having initiated something I wasn't comfortable with, but it didn't matter. I couldn't unsay the words I'd spoken. Once she'd heard me voice such terrible things she began to pull away, to let me go. It would take me years to see the grace in that. At the time it felt invidious.

We still saw each other, though not as regularly and never at my apartment, which would have inevitably begged the question of sex. Pelin stopped sleeping with me once I'd rejected her gift so crudely, once I'd used language to so wound her. Our romance had ended. Instead, we would meet somewhere in public and talk. Sometimes we'd go to a movie and it would take all my willpower not to let my hand sneak over and touch her thigh in the cool dark of the theater. We tried to enact a chaste version of the love and friendship we'd had prior, but the cloud of what happened at the Monteleone as well as my impending departure followed us everywhere. She tried to act excited for me, asking all about New York and my plans, as if she really wanted me to go, and I would roll my eyes and complain about the East Coast, as if I really didn't want to. I felt each grain of sand drop through the hourglass in the time we were together, and I simultaneously cherished them and wished for it all to be over. Part of me desired that when she'd said what she said that day of the letter's arrival—"You must go to New York"—that she'd been possessed of a kind of biblical Adamic language that would transport me there instantly after the declaration.

The slow withdrawal of her from my life was not unlike withdrawal from an addictive substance, or so I imagine. The degrees by which she distanced herself from me, first sexually, then emotionally, were excruciating and painful. And what was worse is that, as the initiator, she was always further along in the process. I was playing catch-up, realizing the pain I felt over our dissolution was not mutual, or didn't seem that way in any case. If only I could have seen that she was tortured by the situation too it would have been a small solace. We would have been going through it together. However, if she'd felt any of the sadness and heartbreak I did, she hid it well or had already faced it down, which made my continued ache all the more persistent and piercing. It had been one thing to lose the physical intimacy we had but something else entirely to lose the emotional intimacy, as well as the myriad quotidian ways we'd wormed into and established a foothold in each other's lives and hearts. I remember the day the cell phone she'd bought me stopped working—she'd cancelled the plan without telling me—and suddenly I began to cry.

One afternoon we met for lunch and I aired some of these thoughts, which to her must have sounded like grievances, the grousing of a spurned lover. I suppose they were. She listened to me and I could see she was growing silently angry despite the stillness of her face. Finally, she couldn't listen to my needy anguish anymore and she cut me off mid-sentence: "You decided to leave me! Remember that before you say such nonsense. I left my husband. It was you who decided to go to New York." That was the thing though: I hadn't really made a choice. Despite what I'd avowed after my encounter with Rostyk, I wasn't brave, for her or for myself, in that moment. I didn't have the dignity of making a hard decision that I knew would hurt someone I loved and owning it. However difficult, at least that would have been honest and respectable. My paralysis and uncertainty had made the decision. I showed her the letter and she assumed I was going, so I did.

We kept in touch for a while after I left New Orleans. I was struggling to adjust to my new life in a new city and would call or write her every week or two. Three months after my arrival, the planes hit the Towers, and I watched the smoke and debris fill the sky for days. Pelin called me frantic, had tried to get through for hours and then days, and she wasn't able to reach me until the 14th. It was only then, when we she finally found me, that I could hear some of the old love creep back into her voice, that love I'd caused her to withdraw from me. "I was so worried, my passion," she said, forgetting herself. She hadn't called me that in months. "Are you okay?" By the time Katrina made landfall, almost four years to the day later, we were no longer in touch. I called and wrote but never heard anything back.

*

On our final day together in New Orleans, we took the ferry to Algiers. I'd never been and regretted I hadn't made more use of the ferryboat. I found it a pleasant ride, the breeze and light coming off the water. We were quiet much of the day, having said all we needed to say to one another. The only thing left for me to do was leave, something I both dreaded and desired. Still, it was comforting to have her walking beside me, to be in her presence one last time. When we returned to the city, it was getting late, to the crepuscular part of the evening when we would say goodbye, and not wanting to let go of her just yet I asked if she'd walk to Faulkner House Books with me, inventing an excuse about needing something to read for my flight to New York.

We walked around the small shop, which would soon close for the day, combing the stacks. That was one thing that hadn't changed: we were both still bibliophiles. In fact, our conversations that last month or so were almost entirely about books. We focused on the lives of other people so as to avoid talking about our own. I found a monograph by a photographer who was soon to be my professor, which Pelin insisted on buying for me. "One last gift," she said. Every kindness could so easily turn into a dagger during those brutal days of our prolonged farewell.

Afterward, we stood outside on the street in Pirate's Alley. We were silent, trying to figure out how to part one another. I noticed a plaque on the wall of the building and went closer to read the inscription. It said that this was the apartment where Faulkner had lived when he wrote *Soldier's Pay*. I'd read a lot of Faulkner at Ole Miss but never that book and said so.

"Most haven't," Pelin said. "It was his first novel. Not very good. He still thought he was a poet."

"I didn't know he wrote poetry."

"There's a reason for that."

I smiled and she nodded, there in the place where we'd met not quite a year earlier, and finally it seemed we had nothing left to say but goodbye. Without looking at her watch she said it was getting late and she should go. We moved to embrace.

"Goodbye, Dixon."

"Goodbye, Pelin."

She neither nodded nor shook her head. I wondered what she felt, what she was thinking. I had no clue and her face, as always, told me nothing. We couldn't draw things out any longer. After all the preamble, the terminus was brief and quick, like a shot administered to induce the death of a beloved family pet. She walked away, no tears this time. I watched her diminish until she reached Rue Chartres, turned, and I could no longer see her.

The following morning I took a cab to the airport. I'd never flown before and wasn't sure how I'd react to being so high in the air. I took my seat and looked out the window at the 737's immense wing. There was a woman sitting next to me, and as we readied for takeoff I noticed she had a music score spread open on her lap. She was playing the piano part with her right hand and turning the page with her left. I wished I could hear what she heard in her head. I assumed she was practicing, for a performance perhaps, but as the plane began to move down the runway her fingers' movements became more intense and agitated, and she exhaled heavily. With one hand she continued tapping out the notes, the other she now moved to her lap, holding fast to the seatbelt. I realized she was scared, that she was playing the music to calm herself. I stole only a quick glance, but I could see it in her face: the expectation, the anxiety, the complete terror as she continued to drum her fingers hard against the thick stock of the paper. Suddenly I felt it overcome me, her fear inciting my own, and

I felt connected to her. I wanted to do something. I wanted to still her hand and say, "I understand." Finally, as we left the runway and rose in the air, I heard her breath catch and she didn't exhale for what seemed a long time. When she finally did let out that soft slow release of air, she closed the music score, put it in her bag beneath the seat in front of her, and leaned back, shutting her eyes. What immense relief I felt. We would be okay. We would live. I took a deep breath and looked out the window, watching as New Orleans shrunk to nothing, and then we were alone in blue, blue sky.

LITTLE AMUSEMENTS

Last September, almost a year ago, I was standing in the street before my house fiddling with my phone, worrying about being late for the benefit, when the car from the ride service arrived. I stepped from the curb and got in, checking the impulse to say hello because I realized that I was the only human inside the sentient machine. All of San Francisco came into view as the car descended from my neighborhood in Bernal Heights to catch the 101 north through Potrero Hill and SOMA into the busy streets and tall buildings of the Financial District. A few minutes later, after being dropped off, I entered the building and checked in. They gave me a badge bearing my name, which I clipped on the breast of my blazer. The room was spacious, with high ceilings and tall windows, and it was crowded with folks holding napkin-swaddled beer bottles or plastic cups of wine, talking loudly at one another to project over the din.

We had all come to support a fundraiser for a woman named Nancy Leventhal, who was soon to be released from prison after spending forty-nine years inside. She'd been a member of a revolutionary cell that attempted to free a comrade from prison. The scheme was botched, however, foiled by an undercover cop who'd infiltrated the group, and everyone was arrested, but not before engaging in a highspeed chase and shootout that left two policemen and one civilian dead.

Behind me, I heard someone call out my name—"Dixon!"—and turned to find Robert Campo waving at me. I walked over and we embraced. Former U.S. poet laureate, Robert had been active in support of political prisoners for decades. I considered him a friend, though the nature of our friendship had vacillated, troubled as it was by the fact that we'd dated for a short spell a few years prior. I'd been the one to end things, amicably enough, but since then I always felt he held our embrace longer than normal to remind me of our former intimacy and his sadness over its demise. When he released me from his arms, he turned to a young woman beside him.

"This is Niko," he said. "We just met, but I can tell she's on the right side of history."

This was how Robert divided the world and identified its inhabitants: they were either on the right or wrong side of history. I took Niko's hand in mine as we yelled introductory pleasantries at one another. There was something about the design of the room that intensified the noise, the yawping echo of speech bouncing off the walls like rubber balls on a racquetball court.

"She just asked about the responsibility of the artist in times like these," said Robert.

"I asked how you saw your politics relating to your poetry," Niko corrected.

"Sure, sure, sure."

"And?" I asked.

"I think there's no separation. My poetry *is* my politics." It sounded nice, a convenient and well-practiced line to convey he was "on the right side of history," and before either of us could respond Robert continued: "It's like I told this interviewer the other day. He asked me whether poetry was a, quote, refuge from the harsh realities of the world, unquote. Did writing poetry comfort me? he wanted to know." Robert paused, looking at the two of us, his audience, as though we'd deigned to ask the question ourselves. "Comfort, I said. In a few months it'll be 2030 and I don't know if we'll make it to 2050. The world is ending second by second. We're all going to be underwater in a few years and he wants to know about comfort. *Comfort?* Listen, buddy, I said, there's something wrong with you if you feel comfortable about anything in the world right now."

Robert is a terrific poet and a terrible blowhard, part of why I stopped seeing him. On the page, the speakers of his poems were more complex and subtle, but off the page, in person, he could easily hold the room hostage for an entire evening with judgments and pronouncements he delivered with absolute certainty. I extricated myself from the conversation, saying I needed to find my husband,

and left the two of them there. I spied him a short while later across the room, Cam that is, my partner, surrounded by a group of people. The overhead lights in the room shone on the smooth skin of his shaved head, giving him a kind of halo, and he waved when he saw me staring, admiring him, but I could tell he was busy, so I did not join. I noticed on the walls were posters and memorabilia on which people could bid with proceeds going to Nancy's release fund. One was a large poster of Lenin in the old communist agitprop style. Another was a collage painting an artist had done of unarmed Black men murdered by police. An 11x14 photograph showed Che in the cane fields waving his machete like a madman. A campaign poster signed by Alexandria Ocasio-Cortez.

I had wandered away from the main room and was standing in a hallway before another item up for auction—a framed issue of *The Black Panther*, the weekly newspaper of the party, that depicted Fred Hampton shortly after he'd been assassinated by Chicago police in December 1969—when the woman I'd met earlier approached me. Niko, I recalled.

"Thanks for leaving me to fall on that grenade," she said.

"Pardon?"

"Your friend. He's…something."

"Oh, Robert. He's just loves talking about his favorite subject."

"Poetry?"

"Himself."

She smiled, and I really took notice of her for the first time in a way I couldn't earlier, when it had been so loud, but here it was quieter, and we didn't have to shout to be heard. She was tall, five-ten I'd guess, and had short Sebergian blond hair. She wore black denim jeans and a black button-down shirt with cuffs rolled to the elbow. The one bit of divergent color in her sable wardrobe was her well-worn white Chuck Taylor high-tops.

"How do you know Robert?" she asked.

"We go way back. I'm involved in the arts, too."

"You're a writer?"

"No, I work in a museum," I said. "I'm a curator."

"Interesting. Do you like it, curating?"

"Very much so. I enjoy working with artists, the living ones anyway. It's gratifying to find ways to present the best version of their work to the world."

There was a large window nearby and through it I spied the Transamerica Pyramid, which refracted so much light I couldn't look at it more than a moment.

I turned back to her, squinting, and asked, "And what do you do?"

"I work for Encounter."

"Really? I've heard interesting things."

"Just moved here from LA last month for the job."

Encounter is a VR company in the Bay that designs adult situations for customers wanting bespoke virtual sexual encounters tailored to their preferred desires. Niko explained that she worked in the development of new scenarios. She found the work creative and challenging. When I told her I'd never tried it, she said that I should, and then we were silent. It seemed our conversation had run its course, though I wanted it to continue. I fumbled for something to say, anything.

"Niko is a nice name," I said finally. "May I ask its origins?"

"It's Serbian, short for Nikolina. That's where I'm from."

I'd detected a slight Eastern Europeanness in her voice and was glad to know the precise nature.

"How long have you been here?"

"Since 2006," she said and thought a moment, adding with a shake of the head, "Jesus, twenty-three years. I've lived longer here than there, hard to believe." She'd been born in Belgrade, she told me, a few years before the start of the Yugoslav Wars that would splinter the country. Or as she said more memorably: "I was born just as my country was readying to die." But Niko and her family stayed and weathered the fighting, bombing, and aftermath before she immigrated to the US for college. She'd spent most of the time since then in LA, at least up until recently, as she'd said, when she moved north to San Francisco for her job. Then, perhaps in part to account for why she was here tonight, she told me that her grandfather had fought with Marshal Tito against the fascists in World War II and that her father had been a relatively high bureaucrat in the Communist Party of Yugoslavia before the republic dissolved.

"Are your parents still there?" I asked.

"Yes, they'd never leave. My father loves Belgrade, though he still says he's from Yugoslavia, not Serbia. He really believed in the socialist utopia, believed in Tito and the nonaligned movement. Both of my parents did, but it couldn't last. You know what my father says about us?"

"What?"

"He says that Serbs are great warriors but terrible soldiers."

I smiled as she took a sip from a green bottle of beer I hadn't noticed she was holding. I nodded at the Black Panther newspaper before us. "A little ironic, isn't it? Selling the anti-capitalist memorabilia of revolutionaries to the highest bidder?"

"It's a fundraiser, not an art auction," she said.

"Fair enough." I was trying to find a tactful way to ask how a new transplant to the city who worked in erotic virtual reality had come to spend her evening at a lefty fundraiser—"So how did you—" when she seemed to read my mind.

"I haven't done anything but work since moving here. My apartment's empty. I had to get out and do something, anything. So I left my place and started walking. That's when I saw a flyer for this and decided to come down. My father will be proud."

"Your father the communist."

"My father the communist," she repeated. "And you? What's your connection to all of this?"

"My husband's father was involved in the incident with Nancy."

"Is he still inside?"

I nodded.

"Still locked up so many years later," Niko said, shaking her head. "'Domestic terrorist' isn't the best thing for a political prisoner to have on his CV these days."

"Robert said that Nancy was just a driver, didn't even pull a trigger. She should have been released a long time ago."

"They're only letting her out to die," I said. "She has cancer. Stage four."

It was true. Cam had told me that was the real reason Nancy had been granted clemency. She'd be lucky to live through the year.

Niko was asking whether Cam's father was ever likely to be released when we were interrupted by someone ushering people into the main room, where one of the organizers wanted to say a few words, and we parted as I went to find Cam. I didn't see her again the rest of the night.

Later, when we were back at our house, Cam and I talked about the evening. We were changing into pajamas, and he'd taken off his glasses. He'd once had long, strawberry-blond hair down to his waist, but on his fortieth birthday, spontaneously, he shaved all his hair off and had kept it so ever since. For simplicity's sake, he said.

"I saw you talking to Robert," he said. "How long did he hug you?"

"For infinity."

Cam laughed.

"He still has a crush on you. It's sweet. Maybe he'll put you in another poem."

It was true. Not long after we stopped dating, I had the surreal experience of seeing myself in a villanelle from his latest volume, addressed as "my gone beloved." I'd made a mistake with Robert. A few years prior, when the museum was planning an ekphrastic exhibition in which nationally renowned poets responded to works in the permanent collection, I'd recruited Robert to take part. Because he was local, he spent a lot of time in the museum and wanted me there to help choose the piece he would engage. One night after working late, I accepted a dinner invitation from Robert that led to sex and then more dates and more sex. Our desire was not mutual, however, and when I broke things off it made the exhibition fraught and difficult. I felt reckless for mixing my personal and professional lives. I'd crossed a line I should never have crossed, one I swore I wouldn't traverse again.

"And that pretty blond woman," Cam continued. "Don't think I didn't see you two off in the hallway talking. Who was that?"

He didn't say this in a way that was the least bit jealous. His tone was playful, inflected with a cheeky admiration. We'd had an open marriage for fifteen years and were honest about our attractions and liaisons.

"Her name is Niko."

"Did you like her?"

"We didn't talk long, but, yes, she was interesting. She works for Encounter," I said, adding, "she's Serbian."

"And attractive."

"Quite."

"Do you think you'll see her again?"

I thought a moment, realizing we hadn't exchanged contact information before parting.

I said, "Probably not" before kissing the top of Cam's head and brushing my cheek against the fresh, smooth shave of his soft skin.

*

The Wednesday after Nancy Leventhal's benefit began, as my Wednesdays typically do, with tennis. I met my tennis partner Tim Tyree at the Olympic Club, where we played on green Har-Tru clay to protect our aging knees. We also play doubles on Sundays with a couple of other men who aren't strong players, just duffers looking for a little fun and exercise, but Wednesdays are reserved for our weekly singles match and the play is quite competitive. On this day, midway through the first set that was even at three games apiece, I served an ace and Tim called out "Foot fault!" from the opposite end of the court.

I looked at him, incredulous. I'd never seen an opponent do that, even in the ultra-competitive junior matches of my youth when we had to officiate ourselves.

"You're joking," I said.

"Nope, I saw it from here, buddy. Your right sneaker was over the baseline. Take a second serve."

I shook my head, muttering abuses, and hit my second serve into the net, gifting him the point that should have been mine. I was furious but determined not to show it as he hustled over to the ad court and began hopping up and down while I prepared to serve the next ball. I imagined the damn thing was a heat-seeking missile that I could rocket into his chest, but rattled by Tim's specious umpiring, I was unable to regain my composure and lost the match.

While Tim and I were tennis partners now, we'd originally connected on an app, each drawn to the other's pictures, as it goes.

But a strange thing happened when we made plans to meet for the first time. I arrived at his place, familiarly anxious yet excited at the prospects of sex with a new person, only to have all the attraction I'd felt looking at his naked pictures dissolve the moment he opened his door. That wasn't the strange part. I'd had this happen a few times before, unwittingly lured into an encounter by someone who'd posted flattering photos of some earlier or altered version of him or herself that bore only a passing resemblance to the person standing before me now. But that wasn't the case here. Tim looked like his photos: a broad-shouldered man with auburn hair and brown pupils. Very handsome. But there was something wrong. It was something else. I hesitate to use the word aura, but perhaps that's what I mean when I say something felt off about him, or me, and us, from the very beginning. There was no vibe, even in the most basic primal, carnal sense. And that's when the strange part of this encounter revealed itself. He felt, I soon realized, exactly the same way.

We talked for a little while, but it was apparent we were both neutral, uninterested, mildly bored, and we began steps to abort our plans in a friendly manner full of no hard feelings. As we said goodbye and I started to walk out the door, Tim said, "Hey, buddy, you don't play tennis, do you?" He looked so hopeful saying it that I began to laugh and even more so when he seemed to find it strange that I was laughing. When I regained my composure, I told him that I had once, in fact, been a very good player—that I'd played D-I in college—but that I hadn't picked up a racket in years. "Oh, come on, please," he said. "I can't find a partner worth a damn here." The strangeness of the moment swallowed me. I found it so droll that I said yes, and we began playing regularly. For so long after college I felt no desire to play, but it has been a pleasure to rediscover my love for the sport. It's a game that's kinder to age than others. We are friendly with one another, Tim and I, but we are not close. None of the digital, ur-attraction that brought us together has ever returned. On changeovers and after matches our conversations rarely go beyond the quotidian realities of work and life, the weather.

That day I recall him telling me that he'd fully committed to a meal replacement drink called Solution. "It's great," he said. "I never have to cook, so I got rid of everything. I have like one plate and fork in my apartment." I thought of *The Jetsons* cartoon from my youth and how citizens of that animated future ate small capsules that contained entire meals. Didn't he miss eating actual food? I asked. "Are you kidding me?" He grabbed a shake from his bag and took a big swig from the taupe bottle. "This stuff is great. It's like the ultimate life hack. I don't even have to think about meals. Wanna try? Go on, buddy." He held it out to me as sweat fell from his arm. I told him no thanks. "Suit yourself," he said. "I should run. See you Sunday?" When he bent over to grab his bag, I noticed the lines of his jock strap had sweat through his shorts, creating the outline of an imprecisely drawn heart, a valentine rendered by an eight-year-old.

After tennis, I returned home and cleaned up, iced a hamstring I'd felt twinge near the end of the match. I had an appointment at eleven a.m. to meet Masha Spitz at a nearby café, so I grabbed my tablet and messenger bag and left the house. As I waited at the bus stop on Cortland, I watched a drone descend from the sky, drop a package on someone's doorstep, and take off again, on to its next delivery. I boarded the bus for the short commute into the Mission District and made my way to Maxfield's, a café Cam and I used to frequent since it was near our first apartment. I was a little early, so I ordered an americano and took it to a sunlit window seat, and before long Masha arrived. She set her bag down at our table—"Be right back"—and went to get a beverage for herself.

Masha is an art consultant. Though she is affiliated with a prominent gallery in the city, she is more of a talent scout and booster for promising artists and makers. There is no one more up on the art scene in the Bay. Periodically we meet to talk about up-and-coming shows and artists. I'm so often preoccupied with the major exhibitions and retrospectives at the museum that I rely on her to keep me up to speed on everything else.

When she returned to the table, Masha began telling me about a series of upcoming shows that would feature artists working in different forms: painting, photography, sculpture, digital and mixed media.

"It's called 'Thirty Under Thirty,'" she said.

I rolled my eyes.

"A bit ageist, isn't it?"

"'Sixty Over Sixty' doesn't sound as sexy, I suppose."

We laughed. The art world's fascination with youth and glamour was symptomatic of the preoccupations of the culture at large, possibly more so.

"So, they're all babies," I said.

"Most fresh out of school."

I groaned.

"They're hungry, as young artists should be," she said. "Don't get me wrong. They're making great work and are happy to be involved with 'Thirty Under Thirty,' the attention it's bringing them…"

"But…"

"But ultimately they have their sights set on something bigger."

She pointed at me, and I turned around as if there were someone standing behind me, which made her laugh. It wasn't unheard of for my museum to purchase and show the work of younger artists, but it wasn't the norm. Usually, artists—even from the elite schools and backgrounds—had to cut their teeth for years, first in group shows and then smaller individual exhibitions, before we ever took notice.

"There are some people I want you to meet," said Masha, taking out her tablet. "I think you'll like their work." She showed me a few of their websites, which were promising, but I can only ever get a sense of the work in person. "Don't decide anything yet," she said. "Just put it on your calendar. Next month, okay?" I trusted Masha and her instincts. Even when they didn't ultimately align with mine, I never regretted following one of her leads, so I told her would be there. "Great," she said, slamming the rest of her cappuccino and looking at her phone. "I gotta run to another meeting—bye!" And like that, she was gone as quickly as she came.

It was nearly lunchtime, so I finished my drink and walked to Bi-Rite, where I purchased a salad and a mineral water that I carried with me around the corner to Dolores Park. I sat and ate and people-watched. I'd planned to head to the museum after lunch, but instead I found myself wandering around the old neighborhood. I walked a couple blocks north to the beautiful old Mission Dolores and turned right on sixteenth. Soon I was standing before the apartment building Cam and I had lived in after we first got together. I squinted through the bars of the gated entryway to see if any familiar neighbors were still affixed to nameplates on mailboxes, but I didn't recognize what I saw. I wondered how much the rent had risen in the decade since Cam and I left, as more and more young tech workers moved into the neighborhood and sent prices skyrocketing. I still remember the angry residents who, resenting the gentrification, would pelt the white Google buses that transported workers south to Silicon Valley with rocks.

I continued wandering the streets, up Valencia and down Mission, noting what had changed and what remained, until I saw the sign above a storefront that had once been an excellent used bookstore. The sign read: Encounter. The U in the word broke from the Copperplate font of the text and was changed into a V that was unmistakably supposed to suggest a vagina. It was garish and tacky, but also, strangely, lent the business an air of pretension, as though *Encovnter* might have been engraved on the oldest building of a prestigious university. I knew there were a couple of stores in other parts of the city, but they must have just opened this one.

I walked inside and found a young man sitting behind a desk, scrolling on the tablet before him. The place had been renovated and restructured to such a degree that I couldn't even recognize its former life as a bookstore. There were chairs in the entranceway, but no one was sitting in them. I didn't know whether that meant business was slow or things were busy in the backrooms where customers would have their VR experiences. Eyes still locked to the screen, the young man said from rote, "Good afternoon. Would you like to have an encounter?"

"Is there someone named Niko here?" I asked.

"I don't know anyone named Niko, sir."

"She works for Encounter," I said. "She designs scenarios."

"That means she's part of Creative, sir, which is a completely different building."

I'd annoyed him, and he was going to "sir" me with unctuous faux respect until I either paid to have an encounter or left him to the scrolling boredom of his tablet.

"Do you know how I could get in touch with her?"

He exhaled long and slow and picked up his tablet. After a few swipes, he turned it to face me. It was a page showing the members of Encounter's creative design team. "This her?" he said, scrolling to the picture of Niko. She was dressed more formally than she had been at Nancy's benefit. Her hair was similarly short, though a touch darker, a sandier blond instead the flaxen hue it'd been the other day. I nodded. There was an email address beneath her bio. I took a picture of it with my phone. "Mystery solved." And before I could say thank you, he added, "You're welcome, sir."

That evening, when I returned home from the museum where I'd been planning an upcoming exhibition with my team, I sent Niko a quick email, saying it was nice to meet her last week and how I'd stumbled onto the new Encounter location in the Mission. *I went inside, hoping I'd bump into you*, I wrote, *but I was told you work in another office.* I'd wished her well, saying I hoped our paths would cross again sometime, and told her to take care. A half hour later I received a text message from a number I didn't recognize. *Hey there*, it said. *Saw your number under the signature line of your email. Hope it's cool.* A few seconds later followed: *This is Niko btw.* I texted back, saying hello. *Did you have an encounter?* she wrote. Cam was still at work, and I laughed, alone at home, sitting at my desk, staring at the screen of my phone. I told her that the only encounter I had was with a snooty person working the reception desk. *Too bad*, she wrote, *you're missing out.*

How about we have an encounter, I wrote. *In real life, that is.*

Sure! What did you have in mind? I haven't explored the city yet.

What would you like to see? I typed. *Don't say Alcatraz.*

Lol. I watched the co-presence bubbles ripple, wondering how I should respond when suddenly appeared: *Show me something you love. Make it a surprise.*

Done. I'm on it, I wrote, and after settling on a time and location to meet we said goodbye.

*

Cam likes to sleep late on the weekends—he can go to the early afternoon if undisturbed—but it's hard for me to go past eight, so I usually get out of bed and make coffee, read the paper, and eventually he lumbers downstairs and joins me. But that Saturday I was to meet Niko at the Ferry Building at eleven, so I made coffee in the French press, set out the *Times* on our coffee table for him, and left a note on the kitchen counter reminding him that I was heading out to meet up with Niko and would be home that evening.

I took the BART to the Ferry Building, where the Farmer's Market was located. It was crowded, but after a few texts I was able to find Niko at the Blue Bottle coffee stand. Again, she was wearing black denim with a dark top, but this time she also wore glasses, elliptical and dark, which I found handsome and well suited to her face. I complimented them. We paused momentarily in greeting before moving to embrace.

"Have you been here before?" I asked.

She shook her head.

"I told you. I've been here a month and basically spent every second either working or getting my apartment set up."

"Where are you living?"

"Japantown. You?"

"I live in Bernal Heights."

"That means nothing to me."

I laughed and said she'd become familiar with the city soon enough. We got coffee and walked through the market, where she bought some vegetables and organic almonds that were spiced with chili peppers. "I have zero food in my fridge," she said. "I've been eating all my meals out." Afterward, we went along the Embarcadero, cut across a few streets, until we came to a steep walkway. "What's up there?" she said, looking skeptical. I told her it was worth it and took the bag from her hands. We walked until the path gave way to a series of staircases and after climbing those, at last we were at the top of Telegraph Hill , staring up at Coit Tower.

"Look," I said, turning away from the white concrete column to face the water behind us, where the San Francisco Bay seemed to stretch forever, container ships dotting the horizon. She was silent, trying to catch her breath, but nodded as she took out her phone to snap a few photos of the sublime view. Then we walked into the interior of Coit Tower and looked at the beautiful Diego Rivera-inspired murals, amused at all the communist references that were sneaked into the artwork. Next I took her to North Beach, one of my favorite neighborhoods in the city. "City Lights!" she said when she saw the great bookstore's façade. We browsed for a while and each bought a copy of the same novel, a new release that had garnered attention, vowing to compare notes.

As we left the store, I suggested we head next door to Vesuvio for a drink and she said that sounded nice. "What would you like?" I asked after entering. "Something refreshing maybe. Prosecco? A mojito?" She looked around at the pictures covering the walls of the unvarnished pressed-tin dive bar. "How about a shot and a beer? Surprise me," she said, then excused herself to use the bathroom. I went to the bar and ordered two Trumer Pils with accompanying shots of Jim Beam. When she returned, she sat in the booth I'd claimed for us and took a quick sip of beer, then reached for the bourbon and lifted it to toast. Something had changed about her, I thought. Her eyeglasses seemed a little different than I'd remembered them being earlier. They looked rectangular now and slightly lighter in shade. When I said something about it, she shook her head, said they were the same glasses she'd been wearing all day, and I didn't give the matter another thought.

By the time we finished our drink—it must have been after one in the afternoon—we were famished. We'd only snacked on the almonds she bought earlier and neither of us had had a proper lunch. I suggested we grab a bite at Café Zoetrope. Housed in the bottom floor of a flatiron-shaped building the color of a long-faded sailor's tattoo, the restaurant is a great place to take a meal. We walked the short distance and were greeted by a hostess, who let us sit wherever we liked. It wasn't crowded. I picked a table by the window so we could watch the theater passing before us in the streets of North Beach. A young waiter arrived to ask what we'd like to drink, and I ordered prosecco and she the same.

"I'm sorry to do this," said the waiter, "but I'm new and they said I have to check everyone's ID."

"No trouble at all," I said, taking out my wallet and handing him my driver's license as Niko rifled through her purse.

Upon looking at my license, the waiter exclaimed: "Wow, you don't look this old at all!" Immediately he was embarrassed and apologized, aware that his remark could easily be taken as an insult instead of the compliment he'd intended. I told him not to worry and smiled. This happens on occasion and it never ceases to be an awkward dance, with the other person trying to make it clear their reaction wasn't a dig at my actual age and me trying not to sound vain when I assure them it happens from time to time.

"How old are you?" said Niko, swiping the license from the waiter, who then left to retrieve our drinks. "Fifty-two." She appraised me a moment, squinting slightly. "I'd have guessed forty-five."

I shrugged, a slight smile.

"How old do you think I am?"

"I know better than to play that game with a woman."

"We're ten years apart."

"I once fell in love with a woman ten years my senior."

I hadn't meant to say it, but my brain just went there, and the words came out reflexively, instantaneously.

"When?" asked Niko.

I thought a moment.

"A long time ago. Almost thirty years."

"Mrs. Robinson," she said, smiling.

"More like Mrs. Rostyk Ozols."

"She was married."

I nodded.

"That must have been difficult."

"It complicated the situation, surely."

"Did you love her?"

"Very much so. I think of her and our time together often."

"It ended badly?"

"For whom?"

"You."

I had to really think before answering.

"Yes and no."

"What happened?" she said. "Tell me the story."

I could see that she was genuinely interested, that she recognized the importance of this older, formative love to me and thus was intrigued, but the story, with all its wounds and joys, wasn't something I felt I could deliver extemporaneously in any kind of coherent narrative, or at least a succinct one, which, rightly or wrongly, I sensed she expected. She would have had to stay seated at that table for three days and been willing to forgive the long pauses and silences I'd need to reflect upon the past so as to be able to not just tell the story but make its meaning. In the end, I downplayed it.

"It's not that interesting," I said. "Her husband found out and that was that."

"Tell me something else then," she said. "Tell me about your husband. What would he say?"

"About me having had an affair with a married woman?"

"Not about that," she said. "What would he say about you being on a date with me?"

"Is that what this is?"

"Don't pretend otherwise."

"Cam would say the same thing about my past affair as he would this date."

"Which is?"

"Which is that's why people should open their marriages. They'd be much happier."

"You're poly?"

I nodded.

"I've had friends who are, but it never seems to end well. How is it working for you all?"

"Good. Great, in fact. It's been many years, so we're well past the growing pains. We'd both been in relationships so badly damaged by infidelity that it seemed to be the only way a healthy relationship, let alone marriage, could work."

"So you sleep with other men—"

"And women."

She cocked her head, raised an eyebrow.

"So you sleep with other men and women."

"Correct."

"How sexually omnivorous of you."

I laughed.

"And your husband knows you're here with me?"

I nodded.

"And he's fine with it?"

"Yes."

"And you? It doesn't bother you to think of him with someone else?"

"Once upon a time perhaps, but not anymore."

I told her that Cam had a lover named Steven whom he'd been seeing for over five years and that I never felt threatened by it. In fact, their relationship made our own bond and sex life better, stronger. I liked him. Sometimes we'd even have a beer together just the two of us.

"Wait," said Niko, throwing her hands down on the table. "You get drunk with the man fucking your husband? What on earth do you talk about?" I must have made a face because she quickly apologized: "I'm sorry, that was coarse. It's just—"

"It's okay."

"It's just, I've yet to meet any couple whose polyamory is nice and neat. It never is. It's always a mindfuck because it's so…so un-societally natural."

"Actually, if you look at the long arc of human history it's very natural."

"I'm not talking about hunter-gatherers and Cro-Magnon free love. I'm talking about the world as it exists now."

"I understand what you're saying, but that doesn't mean it's wrong."

"I'm not saying it's wrong," said Niko. "I admire it. I'm just saying it must be complicated."

"Most human affairs are."

The waiter arrived with the drinks and took our orders, and afterward we talked through lunch about our work.

"I feel ignorant asking this," she said, "but what does a curator do? You pick what gets shown in the museum?"

"Sort of," I said. "It's a big operation. There are five head curators and each of us has several curatorial assistants. We each focus on a different area: Architecture and Design, Contemporary Art, Media Arts, Painting and Sculpture. I handle the Photography collection. There are many aspects to my job. One is building up collections, so I acquire, collect, and catalogue work, but I also try to develop ways in which the art can be experienced and interpreted through exhibitions, events, and presentations."

"Sounds interesting."

"It is, and those are the great parts of the job. The less-great parts, which continue to take up more of my time are fundraising, publicity, and gladhanding with donors."

"What museum are you with?"

"SFMOMA."

"You're serious?" she said. "You're a curator at SF—fucking—MOMA?"

I nodded.

"I thought you were at, like, a small or specialized museum."

It was true that I didn't broadcast the significance of my position. I usually just referred to the institution as "the museum" in a lowercase kind of way. I wasn't trying to be misleading or opaque. It was more that in a profession that too often indulged in—and in some ways was entirely fueled by—self-importance and superficial significance, I tried to refrain from doing so.

"How does that even happen?" she said before I could respond.

"It's a long story."

"I'm not going anywhere."

"I'll try to give you the Cliff's Notes version," I said.

I told her how as a young man I'd wanted to be a photographer and had even gone to a prominent graduate program in New York City. I enjoyed my time there immensely. Having lived my entire life in the Deep South, I fell in love with the city and its cultural bustle. I took advantage of the opportunities that arise when one finds oneself in the art capital of the world: attending openings, going to museums, schmoozing with dealers and collectors, getting drunk with artists and wannabees. I struggled, however, when it came to my photographs. It's not that I didn't take pictures. I certainly did. It's that they never felt like my own. I had my Arbuses, my Winogrands, my Mairers, my Friedlanders, my Robert Franks. God, my sad attempts at Gursky. I was rather proud of some of them until it became clear that I could just about summon anyone's eye but my own.

One day after class, I met with a professor who was an artist I admired more than anyone on that illustrious faculty, whose praise I so desired, to discuss my latest photographs. Often she was generous in her feedback, occasionally fulsome, so much so that amongst my cohort she was referred to as Flattery O'Connor, but on that day her response was measured. She told me that I was like a young painter who trains himself by copying the Old Masters, an analogy I liked until she explained what she meant more fully: "It can be helpful in terms of learning technique," she said, "but it will never be more than an exercise in forgery. Your pictures will not become art until you have fashioned your own aesthetic vision and voice." I wilted in shame and resented her judgment, though I knew she was right. I'd wanted to become a photographer because of the work of other artists, as most do, but I hadn't yet forged an identity that would transcend their influence. I had to face the fact that I struggled to know myself as an artist and that made finding a path forward difficult.

At the same time, I was proving to be an excellent critic and resource for my classmates and their work. Each week during crit a few students would present work for the rest of the class to discuss and provide feedback. Some people said nothing during the entire three hours, others offered thoughtful responses, noting a work's virtues and flaws. But I talked often, at length, and with, so I'd been told by professors and peers, great insight and depth. I wasn't trying to be a nuisance or to dominate discussion; I just genuinely loved talking about art and trying to find ways to help the artist improve the piece or see it in a new way. I became notorious, something of a program legend: the guy who couldn't take a picture worth a damn but who would filibuster a crit into an extended fourth hour. My professors took notice of my gift and recommended me for an internship at *Artforum*, where I gophered for the editors and writers, and which also kept me close to all the action.

Saying this to Niko now, twenty-some years later, I still felt a twinge inside me, my younger self's old wounds surfacing in the fact that I'd not been able to become the artist I'd once so longed to be.

"And then what happened?" asked Niko.

After graduation, I told her, I moved into a tiny apartment in Williamsburg with my best friend Malik. We'd been in the program together—he painted and did video work, what would now be called time-based media pieces—and he was on his way to becoming an art star; he was represented by Gagosian and already had work selected to appear in the Whitney Biennial fresh out of school. I'd left *Artforum* with many contacts and had taken work as an installer while I tried to figure out my next move. I'd been thinking about trying to become a critic when one day I was helping install a group show that Malik was part of. After watching me arrange pieces in a way neither he nor the gallerist had imagined, he told me to forget being a critic, that I should be a curator. Soon I was enrolled in the School of Visual Arts' Curatorial Practice program, and after graduation I went right into working in a gallery. After several years of that I moved to institutions. My big break came when I was hired as an assistant curator at the Museum of Fine Arts, Boston. Eventually that paved the way for me to come to SFMOMA.

I stopped speaking and took a sip of my drink. Niko's mouth began to open, and I could tell she was going to ask more, but I felt I'd been talking too much and wanted to show interest in her life and work, so I asked about her job. What was it like to develop scenarios for Encounter? I'd read stories about the gray-area issues raised by erotic virtual reality, where people could act on their wildest fantasies. Some companies placed restrictions on the types of situations that could be created and purchased, but Encounter was unique in its controversial policy of limitless and uncensored content. I acknowledged that porn has always challenged and indulged taboos—it thrives on them—but what happens when a customer wants to create a scenario involving pedophilia or rape?

"Would you rather they act on those drives in the real world or in a safely controlled environment?" Niko said.

"Apparently at least one customer has done both." I was alluding to an incident last year in which a man paid for a snuff VR encounter and then went out afterward and murdered a woman.

"That guy was mentally ill. You think he wouldn't have killed that woman if he hadn't paid for an experience at Encounter?"

"Who can say?"

"Exactly. Unfortunately, there will always be aberrant situations and people, no matter what restrictions are in place. We can't start legislating morality."

"All laws—and non-laws—legislate someone's morality."

"Maybe. But if corporations giving unlimited donations to political campaigns is considered free speech, then anything we do at Encounter certainly qualifies and does far less harm, in my opinion."

I found the conversation interesting and lively, and when our plates had been taken away, I ordered us Fernet as a digestif. Niko went to the bathroom and when she returned, she sat down next to me instead of across from me as she had during our meal. There was something a little different about her. It was her glasses again. Now they looked more circular and were a slightly different shade than previously. Was it the soft light in the restaurant? I said something about it and again she said they were the same glasses she'd been wearing all day. But when I shook my head—"Am I losing my mind?"—she began to laugh. She reached into her satchel and pulled out four additional pairs of glasses. She said she was doing a home try-on sampling and had devised this little joke on me.

"I tried to hold it together," she said. "I almost lost it when you said something the first time."

Her laughter pleased me, and I said she had a wonderful laugh.

"Did you know that?" I asked. "Has anyone ever told you?"

"No one's ever said so."

"Then I'm glad to be the first."

"What does it sound like, my laughter?"

"First you take a sharp breath in, as if you're surprised to do so. And then it stays there, inside your lungs, like maybe it will dissipate on its own, but in reality it's only gathering strength. Then, suddenly, the laughter comes out of you in one furious deluge."

"Really?"

"Really."

"That's very observant of you," she said, pausing a moment. "Say something to make me laugh."

"Not my forte sadly."

"Please."

I thought a moment.

"Why are most artists starving?"

"Why?"

"Because they have no Monet."

"Oh god," she said.

"See what I mean?"

And that, not my joke but the reaction to my failed attempt at a joke, made her laugh one of her excellent laughs. "See how nice that is," I said, and then added that I'd like to kiss her. "Is that okay?" She stared back at me, her expression unreadable, before finally nodding and I brought my lips to hers.

"Would you like to go to a hotel?" I asked.

"You're forward, aren't you?"

"I'm trying to be up front in my intentions. I'm very attracted to you."

"I know. I could tell the first time we met."

"You could? How?"

"Your eyes, the way you looked at me."

"How did I look at you?"

She smiled.

"Like I was the tasting menu at a three-star restaurant."

I paid the bill, and we walked a short distance to Hotel Boheme. Its lobby was still decorated in bright colors from the Fifties and there were black-and-white pictures of Kerouac and Ginsberg on the walls. I'd stayed there once or twice over the years and its old-world, shabby-chic charm had always appealed to me. There was no elevator, so we walked up the stairs to our room and Niko took a seat at the cabaret table. The space was small in the manner of European hotels, and the smells of buttery pastry and dark-roast coffee filtered up from the café downstairs.

"I love it here," said Niko, taking it in.

"Me, too. They even have complementary sherry in the lobby each evening."

I moved toward her, pulling her from the chair into my arms, and kissed her. I tasted the Fernet on her lips and breath. I started to unbutton her shirt when she told me to stop.

"I'm sorry. Is this okay? I thought—"

"Yes, of course," she said. "But are you clean?"

I said I was, that I was tested regularly. It is part of the rules Cam and I agreed to for our marriage to be open. Niko said she was clean, too, and asked if I had a condom. Of course condoms were another rule that Cam and I had, but I hadn't brought one, so I told Niko that I'd be right back and went to a drugstore down the street. When I returned—I'd sprinted up the stairs, anxious to get back to her—she was lying in bed wearing only her underwear, black boyshorts. She wasn't shy in the least; she seemed completely comfortable with her body. I could understand why. Stating the obvious, I said: "My god, you're beautiful."

She had the long legs of a distance runner. Her nipples were dark, nearly the color of bitter chocolate, and there was a mole just below her hipbone that I wanted badly to kiss, but I stood there frozen, dizzied by the sight.

"Well," she said, "have you decided?"

"Decided what?"

"Whether you're going to come join me or shall I call a cab?"

*

When I arrived home that evening, I found Cam sitting in the living room with our friend Konta and her daughter Ngozi. I hadn't expected anyone to be home.

"I thought you were seeing Steven tonight?" I said, moving to kiss Cam on the head.

"He had to cancel, so I asked Konta to come over. I wanted to see little Ngozi."

I hugged Konta and then bent down to inspect her two-year-old, who was dozing in her bouncer.

"When they're like this, I can almost imagine myself wanting one."

"Like what?" said Konta with a little laugh. "A houseplant?"

"Exactly. Alive and pretty but unburdensome."

"Don't wake her," said Cam. "She just went down."

Konta and her partner Oba were Nigerian transplants, brought to the States from Lagos for tech work, and Konta and Cam have been in the same unit at YouTube for a decade. They are good friends and up until recently the four of us would regularly get together for dinner or to catch a show or some such. However, things had unraveled for our friends in the last year. They'd been trying for a long time to have a child and finally Konta had gotten pregnant, but at six months along she found out Oba was having an affair. When she confronted him about it, he gave her an ultimatum: either they open their marriage or split up.

When I heard about this, I felt somewhat responsible for their predicament. I'd always suspected Oba was envious of Cam and me and our situation, our freedom to see other people, our lives unencumbered by children. Konta, however, wasn't about to go in for something like that and so she left him. Within a few months she was going through divorce proceedings and raising a newborn at the same time, alone, her life upturned so drastically and suddenly. But despite everything, she maintained it was the right thing, was thankful and happy to finally be a mother.

"How was your date?" asked Cam.

"Good," I said, taking a seat next to him on the couch and placing a hand on his leg.

"Tell me about it."

"I don't want to hear about Dixon with another person," said Konta, seriously but disguised in playful jest.

"We tell each other everything," said Cam.

"Let's talk about it later," I said, patting his leg, then turned to Konta. "I'm sorry. We're over-sharers."

"Private matters should remain private," she said. "My mother used to say that." Konta thought a moment, lost in a memory from her past with her now-deceased mother on an entirely different continent. "Although…"

"What?" said Cam.

"I hesitated whether to tell you."

"What?" repeated Cam, his tone inflected with intrigue and worry.

"Speaking of private matters not remaining private," said Konta, thinking to herself. "I found something this morning."

This time neither Cam nor I said a word. We gave her space and time and when she finally spoke, she explained that she and Oba had shared a desktop computer at the house, and it had stayed with her after he moved out. "Today I was looking for a financial file when I came across a document labeled 'Taxes 2.' I didn't remember creating it, so I clicked on it and inside were all these pictures of Oba bound and gagged, being dominated by a mistress. A white woman nonetheless, clad in black leather."

"This was a surprise?" I said.

"Of course it was. I mean, I'd seen his browser history for years and knew what kind of porn he liked. Never anything like this. Bondage? White people? No offense."

Cam and I both raised our hands and shook our heads as if to say: No worries, we don't find ourselves attractive either.

"Our sex life certainly wasn't vanilla," Konta continued, "but this was something else entirely."

"How did it make you feel?" I asked. "Angry?"

"No, not angry. I felt sad," she said, and her eyes began to well. "I felt sorry for him and wondered what I'd done to make him feel like he couldn't talk about something he clearly desired. Obviously that's why he wanted to see other people. But why couldn't he just have told me? Why?"

Cam rose from his chair and embraced Konta. "It's not your fault," he said. "It's not your fault." He looked back at me. "Isn't that right, Dixon?"

"It's not your fault that he couldn't be honest with you," I said, as I moved to put my arms around them. "It's okay, really. It's going to be okay."

*

The following morning Cam woke and came downstairs just before noon. He was wearing a diaphanous white t-shirt and a pair of blue shorts.

"Lazy Sundays," he said, bending down to kiss me. "Is anything better?"

I was sitting at our kitchen table, reading the weekend edition of the *Times* and drinking coffee. His breath smelled bad, but so did mine; we were a united front in halitosis.

"Coffee's in the French press," I said. "You might need to heat it up."

121

When we first started dating, we'd loved sharing the weekend edition of the *Times*, trading sections, chatting about stories we came across. And while we still ordered paper delivery, I mostly now read on my tablet. Cam rifled through the paper, folding and creasing the front page into a manner he liked, but soon he too set it down and reached for his tablet.

I was reading an article about a woman who had killed her granddaughter in what was thought to be the first preemptive homicide sparked by climate change. People had committed suicide as a form of protest, an attempt to spur environmental action and awareness—in fact, the article had begun by referencing the recent spike in suicides among scientists involved in climate research—but this woman had done something different. She'd taken someone else's life. "Climate change isn't coming," read the story, quoting from posts the woman had made to social media before the incident. "It's here and it's only going to get much worse." She alluded to historic "climate events" that had already happened and augured the coming of much worse: famines, heat death, wildfires, drowned coastlines, resource depletion, mass migrations of climate refugees. She ended her post by writing that it wasn't fair for her granddaughter to live through the consequences of a dying planet she and her generation had not cared enough to save. Shortly after posting this, she killed the five-year-old girl, her daughter's daughter.

I found it horrifying, but it moved me as well. I could feel my eyes go humid, thinking about the woman, her despair, and the dead little girl. I'd been relieved to find out on an early date that Cam also did not want children; it was hard to imagine thinking about a child's future through the dark prism of the present. I was about to ask if Cam had seen the article, but he spoke first, motioning toward his tablet: "You won't believe what I just saw. It's awful."

"A new video?"

He nodded.

"It's Sunday—you shouldn't be working."

He shrugged.

"What is it this time?"

"A woman being stoned by her husband and brothers."

"Jesus," I said. "No thanks."

Cam's title at YouTube is Senior Vice President of Content and Monitoring. He heads the team of workers and machines that keeps tabs on what users are uploading and tries to weed out videos that violate the community guidelines. Those with violence, nudity, or copyrighted material are taken down, usually pretty quickly, and AI has developed far enough that it can handle much of the work. But there will always be a need for humans who can work alongside the machines to evaluate content. Some postings fall into a gray area—the sermons of a cleric later cited as an influence by the perpetrators of a terrorist act, for example—and Cam and his bosses have been trying to find the balance between keeping the user-generated content open without letting the site become a refuge for extremism. Given that four hundred hours of content are uploaded every minute, it's a challenge to keep up with it all, to police in real time, even with the help of AI. It also means Cam has to look at horrific images and videos daily, constantly, which accounts for, at least in part anyway, why he's in therapy three times a week and microdosing LSD.

"I nearly forgot," he said, setting his tablet down, "tell me about your date. You said it went well." As I started to answer, the telephone rang. "Great timing, Jerry," said Cam, looking at the wall where the cordless phone was docked. For most of his life he'd had to have a landline so that his father could contact him. The prison required it; cellphones and computers were prohibited, and though there are workarounds now, he has continued to own one out of habit.

"You don't have to answer," I said. "He'll call back."

"I should. We haven't spoken since Nancy's benefit. I'm sure he wants to hear about it."

On the fifth ring, Cam rose from the table, took the phone from its cradle, and walked into the living room. After a few beats of silence, I heard him say, "Hi, Pop."

Jerry had gone to Columbia and joined Students for a Democratic Society, helping organize the famous shut down of campus, and later he became a Weatherman when the group broke from SDS to follow a more militant line of action. He had been a committed revolutionary throughout it all and still is to this day. The jailbreak he and Nancy both participated in happened in 1981, years after most people who'd been underground had surfaced and given up armed struggle, but Jerry was part of the small group who fought till the end.

Even when the action went awry and left three people dead, he remained defiant. Others who were involved had admitted guilt or bargained for lenient sentencing, but Jerry refused to admit wrongdoing, saying, as he still does, that while he regrets three men died, he believes what he and his comrades did was a right and just response to the racism, classism, and imperialism perpetrated by the world's most powerful nation. The judge in his trial was unmoved and gave him three counts of seventy-five years without the chance for parole. Others had accepted responsibility, had admitted it was a crime, had written letters of apology to the families of the victims, had taken their names off the official list of political prisoners, had taken on good works in prison, had filed appeals, had legal teams that rallied public support on their behalf, but not Jerry. He would do nothing to help himself. Of the seven people who were involved, two had died of AIDS while serving their time, three had politically connected families and received pardons, and now that Nancy was getting out Jerry is the only one left inside. I think some part of him takes pleasure in it, in being the last one standing, and it drives Cam mad, his father's obstinacy, his defiance, his inability to take responsibility for a crime that took three lives and left the families of the dead men fatherless. Sometimes they got into terrific screaming matches. "You're not special. What makes your crime more political than a woman who kills her rapist?" I remember Cam yelling at him. "Huh, Pop? Tell me!"

Cam was three when Jerry was arrested and has little memory of their life together prior. Jerry had been long estranged from his parents, so after he went to prison Cam was sent to be raised in a collective of his father's former comrades, mostly women from the movement who had surfaced in Regan's America and were trying to find employment and raise their children while still fighting the good fight, legally now, on a variety of social justice causes and public policy initiatives. Cam referred to these women as his "aunts" and he was very close to them, especially a woman named Rebecca, with whom we always stayed when we visited New York. Cam didn't know who his mother was. Whoever had given birth to him didn't want it known, and no one would tell Cam when he asked, not Jerry, not Rebecca, not any of his aunts. They had sworn never to tell, and they were a group that didn't make promises lightly.

Cam commutes back to New York monthly to see his father. Blood relatives are allowed conjugal visits, which in his case means that Cam can on occasion spend a weekend with Jerry in a small trailer on the prison grounds, talking and watching movies, playing games and cooking meals. I couldn't go on those, but I did tag along on normal visits when possible. I remember the first time I met Jerry. Within minutes of being introduced he asked me about my political affiliations. I said that politics was still relatively new to me.

"New? You're thirty years old. How is that possible? Where have you been all these years, the moon?"

"I was born and raised in Mississippi."

"Jesus Christ," he said, shaking his head.

"It's not something my family ever talked about," I said to Jerry that day. "We were poor. Politics was a game for rich people."

His face was clean-shaven, except for a spot the razor missed at the corner of his mouth. A few hairs sprouted wildly like whiskers on a catfish. He eyed me skeptically. "A man who doesn't know his politics don't deserve to be called a man."

"I'm working on it," I said. "Your son's helping me."

He looked at Cam.

"He'll probably have you knocking on doors for Obama. What a joke. I'll send you some things. Read Luxemburg. Read Gramsci. Read Lenin."

"Can we just have a normal conversation?" said Cam.

"I can do normal," said Jerry. "I can be polite."

He asked me what I did for a living and swiveled toward Cam with a little grin, as if to say, *See, I'm behaving*.

"Dixon's a curator," he said.

Jerry turned back to regard me, the grin gone.

"You hang people's artwork on a wall. How interesting."

"Pop, be nice or we're leaving."

I couldn't hear what they were discussing now, that Sunday morning last September. I washed dishes in the kitchen, put the coffee grounds from the French press into the bin we kept for composting. I went to the bathroom and swiped through profiles on a hook-up app as I defecated. The toilet paper was damp from the steam of my earlier shower. I looked out back to check on the barrel where we collected rain for times of water rationing and drought, and when I walked up the back stairs into the kitchen, I saw Cam standing by the wall, phone at his ear.

"Okay, bye, Pop," he said and placed it in the cradle.

"That wasn't long," I said. "Everything okay?"

"He had to get off the phone because the guards were doing count." It always took something out of him, no matter how short their conversations. The terrible burden of love and blood and history. I rarely spoke to anyone in my family anymore; where I lived now was as foreign to them as what I did. I walked over and put my arms around Cam, asking if he'd like to go out for lunch. "I'd love to, but I rescheduled my date with Steven for today. Is that okay? I can cancel."

"No, don't cancel," I said, and kissed him on the cheek. "Have a good time. Say hello to him for me."

*

I began seeing Niko twice a week, occasionally three if our schedules allowed. We'd meet at Hotel Boheme and sometimes afterward we'd grab a bite to eat at Tosca or Café Trieste or walk over to Chinatown if we were in the mood. Often we lazed in bed, sometimes having sex again, other times just talking. I recall one early post-coital conversation began when she rolled over to face me and asked, "What's your favorite kind of pornography? What excites you?"

I thought a moment, unsure whether to say the truth because it embarrassed me.

"You'll laugh."

"In my line of work, I've seen it all. Believe me."

"Romance novels."

Niko laughed, but it was true. Watching pornography didn't do much for me. Ironic given my profession, I realize, but in this area at least I found the pull of language and narrative to be stronger than image. What I really liked, I told Niko, was going to used bookstores and going through their Romance sections to find books with spines that were heavily creased and pages dog-eared. Part of what turned me on when I read them was the knowledge that someone else had held that very book in their hands and perhaps been turned on. Of course, sometimes the writing in those novels is so bad that the spell is broken.

"Images don't turn you on?" she said. "Like at all?"

"Sometimes, but usually it's not pornography."

I felt that porn had become so prevalent and available and, in some cases, extreme that sometimes simple unexpected images with no erotic intent became, despite themselves, highly charged. For example, I told her, the other day I'd been streaming a television show and an advertisement for a mattress company came on. Normally I muted the commercials or did something else while they ran, but I found myself inexplicably turned on by the sight of a man who was sleeping on his side with one leg beneath the cover and one above. That was it, the positioning of his legs. That was the key to the eroticism of the image. He wasn't wearing anything particularly sexy, just light blue pajama pants, but being halfway uncovered left his right leg exposed and his behind in profile, perfectly scalloped. The image undid me.

"Romance novels and mattress commercials," she said. "If every man were like you, I'd be out of work."

I laughed.

"Who was the first man you ever slept with?" she asked, and before I could answer, she ventured, "Your friend Malik? The artist?"

"How did you know?"

"I could tell from the way you talked about him on our first date."

"Café Zoetrope."

"I knew you loved him, that he was special to you."

"He still is."

It was true. Malik had been kind and understanding in helping me to face down the shame I felt by my desire to be with both women and men. Growing up in Mississippi, I'd learned such behavior was considered so deviant as to be eternally damning. I don't think I even knew the desire existed for a long time because I couldn't let myself know; it was simply a matter of survival. Moving to New York was a revelation, living in a culture, especially the art world, where there was so much more sexual diversity and inclusion. Malik helped me to see and accept that part of myself. After we became friends, he asked me to model for him, and the hours I sat for him in his studio as he painted brought us even closer. He'd never use the word "muse," but I became one of the recurring subjects in his paintings, and I still pose for him whenever he asks. We were never partners—more so dear friends who occasionally slept together—but one of the ways I knew Cam was the person for me was that he and Malik hit it off from the first. I don't know if I would have pursued the relationship if not. That's how much Malik means to me.

"How about you?" I asked. "Do you ever see woman?"

"I used to occasionally. Now mostly men."

I asked if she ever used the VR at Encounter, and she said that she did, that she loved it.

"What do you like about it?"

"I like the options," said Niko. "I can be myself in the scenario, or I can also be someone else if I choose. Any gender, any race, any body type."

"Sounds overwhelming. It's hard enough to know myself."

"I think it's fun to experiment being different people."

"I don't care what your CEO says. Encounter will never create an experience as good as this."

"No?" she said, taking my hand and placing it between her legs. "Like this."

"Yes, this," I said. "The real."

*

Like most couples, we had rules for our polyamory and the foundational precept was open and honest communication, so I told Cam the truth each time he asked about Niko. That is, I told him the truth each time he asked about Niko until I didn't tell him the truth. I did so without forethought, which is not to say I did so without intention. We were at home one evening having dinner, talking about our days, when Cam said he wanted to meet Niko. The request seemed to come out of nowhere; we'd been talking about work.

"What's that?" I said.

"Your lover, Niko," Cam said. "I'd like to meet her."

"Why?"

"Because you're spending a lot of time with her. If she's important to you, then she's important to me. We should know one another." He added after a pause: "Who knows, maybe the three of us can play together."

Occasionally in the past, with previous lovers, we'd done this, invited the other to join, and while Cam liked the overlapping of our marital and extramarital lives, I preferred to keep them separate. I didn't want him to encroach on my liaisons any more than I wanted to encroach on his. We'd had conversations about this in the past that didn't really go anywhere beyond admitting we disagreed on the matter, so instead of pushing the conversation in that direction I did something else. What I said was: "Actually, it's pretty much over. I don't think I'm going to see her anymore."

"Really? What happened? Did you have a fight?"

"No, nothing like that. It was fun while it lasted, but it's run its course."

I'd never lied to him about my previous lovers, and I felt it physically, the untruth, move through me. It wasn't painful; it was strangely pleasing, a bolt of exhilaration shooting through me, a vestige of the old mores being betrayed. I had time to take it back, to come clean as he stared at me curiously, waiting for me to elaborate on the supposed demise of my relationship with Niko, but I didn't, and finally he went back to stabbing his leafy salad. "I'm sorry it's over," he said, then smiled. "Chin up—there will be other little amusements. There always are."

That was how we'd always referred to our liaisons and lovers, as little amusements, an acknowledgment of both their enjoyment and lack of significance when compared to our love.

We continued to discuss other matters as we finished dinner, and afterward I washed the dishes as he relaxed in the living room. Before joining him, I dried my hands and checked my phone. There was a message from Niko asking if we could meet a half hour earlier the following day at the hotel. *Sure*, I wrote. *Can't wait.*

Later that night in bed, Cam kissed me before rolling over to turn out the light on his nightstand. I said, "I love you," as I always did, out of habit, but I felt an immediate rush of relief and gratitude because I knew the words were still true despite what I'd done earlier. I did love him. I loved him so much, could feel the joy and satisfaction of it. This, even as I was betraying him.

*

Early October is a beautiful time of year in San Francisco, bringing our warmest temperatures—summertime in the Bay—and with it this year the "Thirty Under Thirty" show Masha had told me about. In actuality, it wasn't one show but a series of shows taking place in a network of galleries throughout the city, and I'd been going to one each night throughout the week. On the final night, I met up with Masha for a bite to eat before heading over to the Roth Gallery, which was the most prestigious venue involved in the show. These were the artists Masha really wanted me to see, and I understood why after entering. Most of them had been through elite programs at Yale, RISD, Cal Arts, the Chicago Art Institute. The work— mostly painting and mixed media—was technically excellent but still green. It made me recall something I once observed an older artist tell a student during crit: "This is wonderful and terrible all at once, but what's terrible about it can only be fixed by growing up and living in the world a bit more."

There was a large turnout with people sipping champagne and chatting with the artists. I spied Valerie Roth, the owner, holding court, a touch tipsy. Suddenly Masha was behind me, arm on my elbow whispering, "Here's what I really want to show you." She ushered me away from the main room, navigating the crowd, into an ancillary space with fewer people where there was work by an artist named Matthew Smith. Such a plain, unremarkable name, unlike so many artists who were given singular names at birth that seemed to augur greatness. He had not been to a top graduate program in fine arts, I learned from Masha. He was from rural Alabama, the western Black Belt, and kicked around community colleges before graduating from Troy University and enrolling in Auburn's School of Architecture, where he joined the famed Rural Studio program that sent him back to his home county to plan, design, and build homes and structures for under-resourced communities, often using repurposed or recycled materials. He wasn't just an artist; he was a maker, a builder of necessary things.

I was inclined to like him, his story was interesting and uncommon, but the work had to stand for itself, and I was relieved that it did. They were photographs, color, taken with a large format camera propped on a tripod. Most of the images were from Hale County and surrounding areas. The influence of William Christenberry, and thus Walker Evans, was unmistakable, but they were unique in that they incorporated text, each image paired with a sentence or two of sloppily elegant handwriting. Beneath a picture of downtown Newnan were words I leaned close to inspect: *Why haven't you returned my call? The prison only lets me have visitors on certain days.* The neighboring picture showed an old white woman sitting behind the counter of a small country store in which the shelves were nearly bare. The accompanying text: *I promise I won't be mad that you stole my bike if you return it immediately.*

"Now you understand why I wanted you to come?" said Masha.

I was bent at the waist reading Matthew's artist statement when Valerie entered the room with a young man at her side.

"Dixon!" she said. "I want you to meet the artist."

I straightened up to take Matthew in. He wasn't tall, perhaps only 5'8', and he had short dark hair and a mustache. Handsome. He couldn't have been more than twenty-seven, but there was the quality of middle age about him. Experience. He looked like a serious man. He bore resemblance to a young Bruno Kirby, and he did seem to belong to another time. A certain kind of masculinity, which I could only think of as atavistic or anachronistic, clouded off him, but not in a way that was repellent or toxic. In fact, I found myself admiring it. He stood there saying little as Valerie and Masha spoke about his work, and we shook hands. His stoic calm wasn't reticence; it was confidence. He knew he was good. Beneath that equable, self-possessed surface lurked a trace of controlled aggression, a sense that it wouldn't take much to move him to anger or altercation. And yet, his pictures were as sedulously composed as a poet's verse.

"I admire your work," I said.

He nodded the slightest bit, and Valerie said, "He'd be a perfect fit for the exhibition you're planning at the museum."

"How do you know about that?" I said and glanced at Masha who shrugged coyly.

The exhibition in question was one I'd been planning for a couple of years. I envisioned it as a conversation across generations in Southern photography. There would be earlier masters like Eggleston, Christenberry, Sally Mann, and others who put Southern photography on the map, paired alongside work from the newer, more diverse generation of the last fifteen years. It was a pet project of mine, one I'd spent a lot of time trying to get the executive committee and curatorial staff on board with, but now it was set to happen in less than a year's time. Some works we had in our collection, but the bulk I would need to either borrow on loan from other museums and collectors throughout the South or purchase for our museum's permanent collection. This, I could see now, was what Valerie was hoping for.

"I'd like to talk about your work sometime," I said to Matthew.

"How about now?"

I was taken aback by his directness, but I liked it, and agreed.

"Can we get out of here though?" he said, and I sensed the discomfort of this man from rural Alabama in a glitzy affair like this.

"I know just the spot."

"Have fun," said Masha, smiling, as Matthew grabbed his bag and jacket and together we walked outside. I called a car that took us to the Five Hundred Club in the Mission, my favorite bar in the old neighborhood. It was a perfect dive, and I'd spent many evenings there since it was just down the street from the old apartment where Cam and I had first lived. The lighting was dark, the jukebox terrific, and the drinks reasonable. There were black faux-leather booths along one wall and the seats at the bar were only crowded during Giants games. Its neon marquee above the entrance showed a bright retro champagne coupe and martini glass above a sign that says *NOT OPEN 6 a.m.*, an allusion to the days before the city deindustrialized and was full of third-shift bars that workers from the now-disappeared factories and piers lining the eastern coast of the city could hit after working the graveyard shift.

We took a seat at a table in the backroom, and I asked what he'd like. "I don't drink," he said. "Water is fine. No ice." So I went to the bar, returning a minute later with two tumblers, one containing water, the other bourbon. I raised my glass to his, again complementing his work.

"Your voice," he said. "You're from the South, too."

I was shocked he could tell. I'd worked so hard to rid myself of the accent in my younger years.

"Yes, Mississippi."

"What part?"

"Southern, near the Gulf Coast. Hattiesburg and thereabouts. But I went to college up north at Ole Miss."

"Funny to think of Ole Miss as 'up north.'"

Despite his words, he didn't smile or laugh.

I said, "Maybe not so different from how someone in Mobile thinks of Hale County, Alabama. That's where you're from, right?"

He nodded, and perhaps a little too excitedly I started to say, "My favorite book is—"

"*Let Us Now Praise Famous Men.*"

"I guess you get that a lot."

"Yeah."

"Sorry."

"It's fine. I wouldn't be doing what I do if it weren't for Walker Evans's photographs."

"And Agee's text," I said. "You combined the two in a way they didn't. Picture and text together, not separate. Did you write the captions in your pictures?"

He shook his head and told me that they were taken from a local paper in the area. There was a longstanding section called "Voices of the Town," where people could write in to make comments, complaints, compliments—anything really, a community forum in print. It was making sense to me now. I'd found some of the captions humorous, others devastating. There was a quotidian poetry to them that matched Matthew's photographs perfectly. He told me he'd spent a lot of time in the archives going through years and years of the paper, trying to find the right comments to accompany specific pictures. His voice was soft, almost hard to hear. I had to lean forward across the table. The more I listened to him I could tell from the timbre and volume of his voice that there wasn't anything weak or effete about it. It was the voice of someone consciously trying to control it because he wasn't naturally soft tempered.

"Fascinating," I said when he was finished. "And you're represented by Valerie?"

"Yes. For now, anyway."

"What do you mean?"

"She hasn't sold much," he said. "Or anything really besides a few small pieces. She believes in me, but she also believes in making money."

Most gallerists have their artists who pay the bills, those who bring prestige or credibility, and those who might be called sleepers—artists the dealer hopes will ascend to one of the other categories. Matthew was a sleeper, and he was right about Valerie. However great the art, the big players all answered to a bottom line. I knew Valerie well; she'd drop him if his work didn't start selling.

"Hence 'Thirty Under Thirty,'" I said.

"God, if I have to hear that one more time."

"They should have just put your birth certificate up on the wall instead of your artist statement."

For the first time in our conversation he smiled but with reticence, as if it pained him to do so.

"What's the exhibition you're working on that Valerie mentioned?"

I told him the general idea, concluding: "For so long I'd hated where I'd come from and had only been able to see it as a cultural backwater. Real art couldn't possibly come from the Deep South. Ironically, it took fleeing the region and going to New York to be able to see its beautiful complexity. I want to bring that to San Francisco, to others who might only see the South through the lens of regressive politics and awful headlines in national news outlets."

"Good luck with that," he said, which almost made me laugh-spit my drink across the table.

"Tell you what," I said and wiped my lips with a cocktail napkin.

"How about we schedule a studio visit? Have Valerie contact me to set it up."

"Really? You'd do that?"

"No promises of course, but I'd like to take a look."

"I'll call her tomorrow," he said, and thanked me.

*

On a weekend when Cam flew to New York to do a trailer visit with his father, I found myself driving over Golden Gate Bridge in the late evening, past the Marin Headlands, and into the Russian River Valley. Before he'd left for the airport, Cam finished packing his bag and stood before the open door of the bathroom. I was inside at the sink, naked, grooming myself. "I like to watch you manscape," he said. He'd shaved his head earlier and there were still little bits of his hair peppering the sink. Now mine commingled with his. He studied me in the mirror as I ran the razor over my scrotum, lathered with conditioner. "What will you do with yourself this weekend?" he asked. Originally, I thought it would be an opportunity for Niko and me to do something, perhaps get out of the city and go to Monterey or Big Sur, but Malik had called to say he'd be in town, and I never missed an opportunity to see him. "Oh good," said Cam. "It's been a while. Give him a hug for me."

Malik's gallery and studio are in New York, so he lives in a massive loft in Red Hook, but a few years ago he purchased a cabin on the Russian River that was both a place to vacation and a reason to see me. I loved it when he came to town and we'd escape to the woods for a nice slow weekend on the water, just the two of us. The cabin had nearly been destroyed in a wildfire the previous year that ravaged the valley but thankfully survived.

I hadn't seen Malik since early August. He'd had a much-acclaimed solo show in Chelsea that fall and I felt bad that I'd not been able to make it. We weren't great at keeping in touch, but we always tried to see one another when possible and when we did, it was as though the time and distance we'd been apart evaporated.

I arrived just as it was getting dark. I could see the light on in his cabin. I knocked and there was no answer, so I let myself in. His bags were strewn across the living room floor. I called out his name, but there was no answer. I dropped my overnight bag and walked through the kitchen to the back part of the cabin where there were two rooms: one his bedroom and the other his studio. I peeked into the latter and saw an empty easel and a cluttering of abandoned canvases. That left the bedroom, which is where I found him, asleep in his bed.

Malik was under the top sheet but his upper half, shirtless, was exposed. He is a little older than I, having just turned fifty-three, and he'd put on a little weight since I'd last seen him, but it looked good on him, his little belly and big chest. His hair was dreaded, as it had been since we met, but it was longer now and fanned all over the bed. His skin was very dark except at his hands and forearms, which were almost entirely white, due to a melatonin condition. That was the only place where it manifested, and he'd once told me that as a boy it had so embarrassed him that he'd taken to wearing elbow-length gloves to school until the other kids called him a woman and a fag, and he decided that it was easier to take the abuse directed at his pigmentation than that directed at his gender and sexuality. He didn't like to talk about his past; his childhood had been too dark and painful. From the beginning, I'd sensed something almost chthonic about him, as though he'd experienced some great catastrophe and his presence here in this world was only ever a visitation from that other one, that place of sorrow beyond dreams that sometimes surfaced in his paintings.

Suddenly one eye opened, inspecting me, and the other followed. Smiling now, he donned his black-framed glasses.

"What are you doing?" he said.

"Watching you sleep. I just arrived."

"Sorry, I was waiting up, but the jetlag caught up with me."

"Don't be. I wish I could have made it sooner."

"What were you thinking?"

"When?"

"Just now. When you were watching me sleep."

"That you are beautiful and if I had any of the gift you have, I would try to paint the image so I could have it forever."

"You cheeseball," he said, laughing a little laugh. "Besides, you're the only one who'll be painted this weekend."

Every time we met up, he'd do a portrait of me. It was a tradition, something he liked to do, almost from the beginning of our friendship. I'd let him, even though it made me self-conscious. Last year Cam and I visited his studio when we were in New York to see Jerry and Malik showed us a dozen or so paintings he'd done of me over the years. It was surreal to see so many versions of myself lined up. Most were direct portraits done throughout my late twenties, thirties, and forties—the nearly three decades I'd known and loved Malik—but that day I found out he'd begun doing paintings that were imaginations of me as a younger man, a boy even. They were based on stories I'd told him. "A collector's interested in that one," he said, pointing to a large canvas that showed me—not more than seven—walking through the piney woods of rural Mississippi, where I'd grown up.

"How much is it going for?" asked Cam.

"Ninety."

"*Thousand?*" I said.

"That's a bargain. Guy's a friend of Larry's," he said, referring to his dealer.

He smiled at my incredulousness. It wasn't that I was unfamiliar with the prices Malik's work could command. It was that I couldn't imagine anyone paying that much for something bearing my likeness. At first it was just something done for fun, but somewhere along the line it became serious and now "the Dixon paintings," as they'd come to be known, were showing up in auction houses and in the collections of serious buyers. How strange, how utterly bizarre, to imagine myself in a museum or private collection on canvas instead of in the flesh.

Now in bed at his cabin, he sat up and told me to come to him and I did. "Hello handsome," he said, and we embraced and then kissed. "Make yourself comfortable." I took off my shoes, then my clothes, and got under the covers. We lay side by side, naked.

"Did you fly in from New York?" I asked.

"Budapest."

"What were you doing there?"

"I had," he said, yawning as he waved his hand toward the ceiling, "a thing. You've been to Hungary?" I shook my head. I was lying on my stomach, listening to him talk, and he pulled back the sheet covering us. He ran his hand down my spine to my tailbone. "Budapest is a great city. Actually, it's two cities. There's Buda," he said, squeezing one of my butt cheeks, "and Pest," as he moved his hand to the other. I smiled as he dragged a finger along the crack between the two. "And between them flows the Danube."

I told him I missed him, and he leaned down to kiss me, good and long.

*

It was after Thanksgiving when I finally heard from Valerie. I'd been so busy at the museum, helping close one exhibition and preparing to start another, that I'd practically forgotten about the invitation I'd extended the previous month. Then one day there was an email from Valerie in my inbox: *Sorry for the delay, Dixon—he just told me about your conversation at Thirty Under Thirty! Matthew's the real deal. How about a studio visit this week?*

We made plans to meet at Matthew's atelier in Dogpatch a few days later, and when I arrived, I found that he'd set out twenty of what he felt were his strongest works, but there were stacks of others. I stayed through lunch, looking at them all, not wanting to stop until I'd inspected every piece. There were at least six I was seriously interested in acquiring for the museum, and one I desperately wanted for myself. I purchased that one on the spot, but the others I'd have to wait on, as it wasn't my decision alone. I couldn't do whatever I wanted with the museum's money. I'd need to talk to my staff and the executive committee to get them on board, as well as the trustees, but I was excited at the prospects of this young talent. It would be great to have his work in the permanent collection now before his prices skyrocketed the way Malik's had as a young artist after he'd started to gain recognition.

When I met up with Niko the following day, I was still under the spell of Matthew's work and couldn't stop talking about it. This was a rare time that we met up somewhere other than the hotel. I suggested we have a picnic lunch in Delores Park. It wasn't far from her workplace, and I picked up food and drink around the corner at Bi-Rite. We were sitting on a blanket on the high hill of the southwestern edge of the park, drinking small aluminum cans of blanc de blanc and spreading brie and chevre on hunks of torn baguette. Niko brought a jar of delicious jam her mother made from rosehips, as well as one containing a roasted red pepper relish called ajvar, a Serbian specialty, that I was quickly becoming addicted to. I'd gone vegetarian in my thirties, but Niko was an omnivore, so I'd picked up some soppressata for her. I enjoyed watching her dangle it into her mouth, remembering the savory salt and spice. I would taste it on her lips later when we kissed.

I went on about Matthew's work, recounting certain photographs and their accompanying text, and Niko listened, smiling at my excitement.

"And you should see the one I bought for myself," I said. It was a landscape of a cotton field in lay-by season, the hoeing, planting, and cultivating done. Just the blackest dirt you'll ever see. And in the far distance, easily missed at first glance, appear to be two children playing in a broken-down car. The accompanying text read: *To the girl working the register at Dollar General on Thursday May 11, thank you for being so kind and smiling at me.* I'd taken it home that night to show Cam. We'd spent the night sipping wine and figuring out where to hang it in our house.

"Can I see them?" Niko asked. "The photographs."

I pulled out my phone and brought up Matthew's website, but it was inferior to experiencing the work in person. I heard Niko say "Hmm," followed by "it's nice," which felt like a blow after my assertion of its excellence. She dropped the bit of cheese she'd been about to eat onto her plate but said nothing. We were quiet, and I remembered something I'd thought of the other day when I was in bed next to Cam but thinking about her.

"Do you know Brillet Savarin?" I asked as I reached to break off another piece of bread and dunked it into the rosehip jam.

She shook her head.

"He was a French lawyer and politician, but he's remembered today for his writings about food."

"What about him?"

"He believed there were six senses. In addition to the five we know, he thought physical desire was another and that everything

139

wonderful about the first five was due to the sixth, to, quote, 'the desire, the hope, the gratitude that springs from sexual union.'"

"What is it you like about me, Dixon? Is it just the sex?"

I was taken aback by the change in tone, her asperity. I could tell she'd been waiting to ask this as I prattled on about Matthew and his pictures.

"No, not just," I said. "Though it is wonderful."

"But what is it you like about me?"

"I think you're intelligent and creative and funny. I enjoy our conversations. And surely you know I find you beautiful."

She said nothing.

"I like that you're independent and seem capable of anything put before you." I recalled what Robert Campo said when he introduced me to her. "I like that you're on the right side of history. I love your terrific laugh."

"Would you ever leave your husband for me?"

"No," I said without hesitation, which was the truth. "Cam is my primary. I couldn't leave him. I wouldn't want to."

"I appreciate your honesty." She said this without a trace of hurt or defensiveness. "It's just sometimes I wonder what a life together could be like if it were allowed to exist outside a hotel room in which we only had sex. Our relationship might take on new dimensions we're not able to explore now."

"Hey," I said, smiling as I reached to touch her arm. "Look at us. What hotel? We're in a park and actively not having sex. Look how chaste we're being."

She half-smiled at me, but still I saw it, the hurt.

"Do you want to stop seeing each other?"

"No, I don't want to stop," she said. "But I'd like to have an actual relationship at some point. I might need to start seeing other people. People I can actually date."

"Of course. I told you from the start to see whomever you wanted."

"I wanted to see you."

"I'm sorry. This is what I can give."

I was still deceiving Cam about Niko. Initially it had been driven by a desire not to have to share her with my husband, as he hoped, but something had happened in the weeks afterward when I'd come home from seeing Niko and tell Cam all about the tennis match I supposedly won or the meeting I claimed to have suffered through that afternoon at the museum. I was coming to realize that part of the attraction and energy in my relationship with Niko *was* the lie. It excited me. Furthermore, I was able to do so with less damage to my conscience because the deceit felt somewhat innocuous, unnecessary even. We were both allowed to see other people and so I was. By opening our marriage, we felt we'd conquered the negative externalities of the old morality—jealousy, covetousness, dishonesty, boredom—and yet here I was behaving this way. Was I nostalgic for something I supposedly despised, had allegedly overcome? I wasn't sure. I couldn't fully fathom my own heart, my intentions and desires.

"I have an idea," I said. "Cam has a work trip in Asia after the holidays. What if we went somewhere? Big Sur? Monterey? We can fly to LA or Palm Springs. We could go anywhere. What sounds good to you?"

"I don't want to go anywhere. We're already in the most romantic city in the country. Show me something I've never seen before."

We both smiled, remembering the catalyst of our first date. I still recalled her text: *Show me something you love. Make it a surprise.*

"I have a few ideas."

"Good," she said, and we both sat quietly, looking around the park at all the people there in the middle of a weekday. There were young folks everywhere.

"When will it all end?" said Niko. For a moment I thought she was talking about us, our relationship, but it didn't seem so. She wasn't looking at the people in the park; her line of vision was directed out toward the water of San Francisco Bay. I asked what she meant. "This city. How long before it disappears under rising sea levels or breaks off from the rest of the country when the Big One hits?"

"Sometimes I feel like it already has."

"Dixon," she said.

I was thinking about the end of the world, and it took me a moment to return to the present.

"Dixon?"

141

Still I said nothing and I felt the power of her stare on my cheek until I turned my vision away from the water to meet her eyes. She stared at me for three full seconds, a strange inscrutable expression, before shaking her head.

"Go on," I said. "I'm here."

"It's nothing," she said, looking into my face without looking into my eyes.

"Please."

"Never mind." She picked a few spears of grass from the ground and threw them fluttering into the air. "I've already forgotten."

*

I didn't see Niko during the holidays. She went back to Serbia to visit her family for two weeks, and Cam and I traveled to New York to ring in 2030 amongst friends and family, to see Jerry. When we came to the city we always stayed with Cam's "aunt" Rebecca, who'd been in the movement with Jerry and who had helped raise Cam when he was young and living in the collective. Of all the people who'd been around in those days, Rebecca was the one to whom Cam was closest. After Nancy Leventhal was released from prison in the fall, she'd moved into Rebecca's apartment in Morningside Heights, and Rebecca was doing her best to tend to her sick comrade. There was no question of the cancer getting better; it was how quickly it would worsen. Still, she was in pretty good spirits, happy to be on the outside, even infirm, after so many years behind prison walls.

It was difficult for Nancy to get in and out of bed, so in the evenings we'd gather around her and talk, as old friends dropped in to say hello. One night, when it was just Cam and me in the room with Nancy, I asked her if there was anything I could do for her, anything she needed. Would I mind rubbing her hands for a minute, she said. "They're sore. I don't know what the hell that means. Do I have arthritis?" I said I didn't know but was happy to and moved to sit on the edge of the bed, taking one of her hands in mine. When I began to massage, she closed her eyes and tilted her head back, exhaling hard in a groan of pleasure-pain.

"Do you know how long it's been since anyone's touched my hands like this? I can't remember the last time." I watched her,

142

the creases and wrinkles on her face contracting and expanding. "Harder," she said, and I applied more pressure. I continued to rub her hands until my own ached, but I wouldn't stop.

"I need to ask you something," said Nancy. For her pain she was taking a medication that left her mouth dry, so she was constantly smacking her lips, trying to create saliva.

"Go ahead," I answered.

"Not you," she said, turning away from me toward Cam. "You."

Cam left his seat and came to the bed, taking Nancy's free hand. "What is it?"

"Why do you shave your head like that? You look like Yul Brynner."

"I think he looks handsome," I said, but Nancy shot me a silencing look.

"It's just simple and easy. No hassle," said Cam. "I don't know. Maybe I'll grow it back out at some point."

"And why did your father give you a bourgeois name like Cam? I never understood. It makes you sound like you never leave the country club."

"It's short for Cameron, my grandfather's name."

"Oh."

"I'm lucky he didn't name me Trotsky."

Nancy smiled briefly and then apropos of nothing she announced: "I'm going to die soon."

Cam made no pretense of denial or brightsidedness. He said, "I know."

"Your father and I go way back."

"I know."

"Not just the thing we did. Our crime. Before that."

"I know. He's told me."

"Way back to when we were Democrats, just ignorant kids. We didn't know anything. We met freshman year right down the way at Columbia. He liked me, always had, from the beginning. He said I was the smartest, toughest woman he knew. I liked that. We all slept with a lot of people, everyone in the movement. We had no interest in marriage, none of us. Smash monogamy and all that. But some did want children, a kid or two maybe. Your father was one of them. And since he thought I was the smartest, toughest woman he knew, he asked me to bear his child. I told him no. I was gay after all. Besides, I don't want children, I said."

I was still rubbing Nancy's hand but watching Cam's face. I could see him realizing what was happening. We both were.

Nancy continued:

"He kept asking and asking until I finally agreed. But I told him I had one condition."

Cam neither nodded nor spoke. We were both frozen, as though any movement we made might prevent Nancy from finishing her story.

"That afterward I not be asked to do *anything*"—her finger sliced through the air as though it were a military saber—"and that the child not know I was its mother. I didn't want the responsibility or obligation. I was trying to bring the war home in the belly of the fucking beast. What did I want with kids? I wanted to give birth to the revolution." Cam began to cry. I let go of Nancy's hand and moved toward my husband. "I didn't want to be anyone's mother, but here I am dying, and I don't want to die with secrets. I wish we'd...I don't know. What has your life been like? Tell me." Cam lowered himself to the bed to embrace Nancy. I no longer belonged there, so I walked away quietly and joined Rebecca in the other room.

"She told him?" said Rebecca, pouring red wine into a glass.

I nodded.

"Cam always thought it was you, that that's why you're so close."

"Well, now he knows the truth. Thank god. One more secret I'm no longer burdened with."

*

After Nancy's revelation, Cam was furious with his father. He'd long been resentful that Jerry hadn't told him, but that was an anger he'd grown accustomed to and had accepted so that it was familiar enough for the pain to dull into disregard. It was another thing entirely to be told the truth now, especially as his mother was dying. We left New York without visiting Jerry again and when we returned home Cam wouldn't answer his calls. Nancy, on the other hand, he talked to each night on the phone. He wanted to know what little time allowed of this stranger who'd given birth to him.

"How is Nancy?" I asked one night in bed after Cam had finished his nightly call to New York.

"Worse. She's in a lot of pain."

"I'm sorry."

"I would have hated her, you know."

"What?"

"As my mother," he said. "If she'd raised me. We would have never stopped fighting."

"Do you wish she hadn't told you?"

His face warped into something abject.

"Of course not. I just wish I'd known forty years ago. I might have actually been able to have some kind of relationship. Not whatever this is."

Nancy's revelation changed something in me as well. I saw my behavior with Niko in a new, if obvious, light: selfish, hurtful, devious. I knew those things about myself, but now I felt them in a way I hadn't before. How could I keep lying to my husband about Niko for the sake of my erotic titillations and game-playing? Why would I ever sabotage a life and partner who made me happy, a life and a partner I loved? I wanted to be a good husband again. I wanted to support Cam in this difficult time. I had to stop something I should have never started. And yet. Three times I went to meet Niko at our usual time and place with the full intention of breaking things off and each time, at the decisive moment, my resolve crumbled. By the fourth meeting, our affair felt familiar again, part of the sense of normalcy in my life, and the urgency to end things dissipated.

*

When Cam's work trip to Asia came, I decided to take Niko to Malik's cabin in the Russian River Valley for the weekend. It felt like a betrayal to the two most important men in my life, but I'd become good at compartmentalizing my emotions and guilt. Having only experienced the city, Niko was thrilled to get out in nature, to hike and dip our toes in the cold, cold water. I had fulfilled her wishes in showing her something new. We built fires and cooked simple meals over them, then spent the night making love and cuddling under heavy blankets, sleeping until sunlight came through the windows and woke us.

It was disappointing when we had to return to civilization. There was little cell service in the valley, and it had felt good to disconnect from real life, but it beckoned, as it always does. The Sunday evening before Cam was to return, I had an appointment to meet Matthew to discuss the acquisition of his work. I wanted to keep it informal, so I didn't involve Valerie, and arranged for us to meet at Tosca in North Beach. On the drive into the city, I asked if Niko wanted to join, to meet this young artist I was so excited about, and she said yes.

We arrived a little early and took a seat in the lounge. I ordered a Peroni for Niko and a Negroni for myself. When Matthew arrived, I rose to shake his hand, and introduced him to Niko. I didn't designate the nature of our relationship—it would have been absurd for me to say, "This is my lover"—and I wasn't going to lie and say she was my assistant or some such nonsense. It was clear enough we were there together as a couple of some sort, so I just said, "Matthew, this is Niko."

For a moment he looked hesitant, as though he might not be comfortable with her present, but then he took his hand from his trouser pocket to shake hers.

"What can I get you to drink?" I said. "There's a cocktail list."

"Just a club soda," he said. I'd forgotten he didn't drink, so I asked if he'd like some food or dessert, but he declined, no thank you.

I went to the bar to get his club soda, and when I returned, Niko was ebullient—lips curved into a warm smile, her head nodding encouragingly—as she listened to Matthew tell the story of how he went from the Black Belt of Alabama to being represented by the best gallery in San Francisco. I felt a certain kinship with him: both of us from the rural Deep South having found our way out and worked our way up in the elite and cutthroat world of art. He was, as I remembered, very handsome. I sensed from her smile and energy that Niko thought so, too. For a moment I imagined the three of us making love together and then just me and Matthew. I had fantasized about that once or twice after I visited him in his studio, but it could never be more than that, an innocuous daydream, as his work was now a potential addition to the museum. I'd learned that the hard way with Robert Campo never to mix business and romance.

I asked how long he'd been in the Bay.

"I left Alabama three years ago."

"Do you miss it?"

"Not particularly, but I might need to move back."

He was having trouble finding steady work, he said, having to rely on odd jobs to get by.

"Does it leave you any time to make pictures?" I asked

"Not as much as I'd like. But I get up at four to work for a few hours before the day starts and again at the end of the day."

"That's the kind of discipline an artist needs," I said.

"Would you ever consider teaching," asked Niko. "Many artists do."

"I'd rather die," he said. Niko and I laughed but Matthew didn't. "Besides, I'm not exactly the kind of demographic hiring committees are looking for."

"What do you mean?" asked Niko, and Matthew held up his hands as if they were covered in blood.

Niko laughed at the gravity of the gesture.

"I'll be sure to shed a few tears later for the plight of the privileged white heterosexual man."

Now I laughed and Matthew's gaze whipped from Niko to me, menacingly.

"How?" he said, turning his attention back to her. He leaned forward across the table. I could sense him trying to control the timbre of his voice, to restrain the intensity and resonance with which he might normally respond. "How do you know I'm privileged?"

"How do I know you're heterosexual?" said Niko.

I placed a hand on her leg, silently urging caution, as Matthew's eyes widened a little.

"How am I'm privileged? What do you know about me? I just told you where I come from."

Niko's smile dissipated and she stared at Matthew a moment.

"And look at where you are. You're a white man with a good education. You have a graduate degree."

"I have thirty grand in debt."

"You have work that is attracting attention and being shown in a significant gallery."

A tension had come into the conversation after Niko's barbed joke, but I didn't intercede. I liked that she wasn't afraid to voice her thoughts and that she could swing back when Matthew challenged her. Matthew sat silent, though I could tell he was nettled, and when Niko started to speak again, he cut her off by changing the subject: "And what is it you do?" When Niko explained about her work at Encounter, Matthew said nothing, just regarded her as though she'd said she was an accountant who played with an abacus all day.

"Not exactly the high art you do," she said, "but it is a creative outlet."

"There is no high and low art," said Matthew. "Only the process of making."

"I disagree," said Niko. "I think there's a difference between work shown in a gallery and the work I create to get people off."

"There's actually no difference," said Matthew. "It's a perfect metaphor in fact."

I laughed.

"But it's the intention, no?" Niko looked from me to Matthew. "I make art—if you must call it that—simply for a paycheck. Presumably you make art for another reason even if your work is eventually sold." She paused, waiting for him to answer, and when he didn't, she asked, "I mean, what is art anyway?"

"A survival strategy," said Matthew immediately.

"I used to think art was a tool the universe uses to become aware of itself," I said. "Now I see all art as a theory about what art can be, whether that's erotic design scenarios or fine art photography."

Money is one of the knottiest aspects of the profession, I told them. It simultaneously keeps our whole world afloat and debases everything about it. I recalled how over the years I'd been approached by tech millionaires in Silicon Valley wanting to lure me away from the museum to manage their private collections, but I'd always turned them down even though the money I could make as an art advisor was far more than I made as a curator.

"Why?" asked Niko.

"I suppose I like the way that once a museum purchases a work of art it takes it off the market and into the public good, making the piece both priceless and utterly valueless."

"But it's not like the museum is some holy institution operating outside the reach of capitalism. Do you know where your donors' wealth comes from? What's funding the expansions, the exhibitions, the new wing? And as far as the work itself, it takes money, often quite a lot of it, to acquire a piece, to make it become 'utterly valueless,' as you say," said Matthew, not a little pointedly.

He was right of course. I knew all of this, as well as my own Pollyannish tendency to romance the role of the museum, and thus my place in it. All I could say was: "Well, it's not a perfect situation, is it."

His response was also a reminder of why we'd set this meeting in the first place, to discuss the possible acquisition of his work. Before doing so, however, I asked Matthew why it had taken him so long to set me up for a studio visit with Valerie. What I had come to think of as his normal affect, at least in the little time we'd spent together, seemed to connote an amalgamation of attitudes: confidence, obstinacy, melancholia. Only when I asked this question did I sense something else in his countenance, a vulnerability, a hint of doubt.

"I didn't think I could take another rejection," he said and sipped from his drink. "Or worse, a close call. I've had several. Studio visits with excited collectors who leave saying they'll call but never do. If it happened again, I thought I just might give it all up and move back to Alabama to work as a carpenter."

"Well, I can't have you doing that now. I'm sure Valerie has told you that I'm quite fond of your work. I can see it fitting in well at the museum."

"Then why haven't you made an offer?"

I explained the lag. It was different than a collector who could whip out a check book on the spot. With an institution there was a whole process to acquiring work and it tended to be glacial; a lot of people had to sign off.

"No promises," I said. "I still need the OK from the higher-ups, but they usually let me take on the work I choose. I want to make sure everyone at the museum is on board. I want there to be an excitement about your photographs. They deserve it."

"Yes, they do," agreed Niko.

Matthew looked at her, finally softening. Half of his face smiled. I excused myself to use the restroom, and when I returned Niko and Matthew seemed to have forged a pleasant enough truce. We talked for a while longer, the tension eased, and before long we parted. Niko and I walked the chilly streets of North Beach, an area of the city that I'd come to associate with our relationship since we rarely left its boundaries.

"He's an interesting one, isn't he?" I said of Matthew.

"God, he's intense."

"I suppose that's why his photographs are so strong."

We walked on and after a few beats of silence Niko said, "He asked if he could see me tomorrow night."

"Matthew? When did he say that?"

"While you were in the restroom."

I didn't know whether to be offended or impressed.

"That's some dash," I said. "It's obvious we're here together."

"I know."

"What did you tell him?"

"I told him I couldn't. I have a work thing."

"Would you like to see him?"

"This weekend has been special. I just want to be with you."

I took hold of her hand and it felt good to do so. We tried to maintain a modicum of discretion in public, but tonight I stopped and turned to her under the awning of a café and kissed her flush on the mouth.

*

Shortly after Cam returned from New York, I dreamt about him and Steven. It was purely domestic, nothing sexual. Just them living together in the same home Cam and I share in Bernal Heights. They were having dinner and afterward they sat on the couch and Steven rubbed Cam's feet as they watched a movie, as I often do. I was nowhere to be found in this conjugal tableau. In the logic of the dream, it wasn't that Cam had left me to be with Steven. It was as though I'd never existed, and Steven had simply assumed a role that had never been mine to fill. It was a strange kind of meta-sleep in which I was aware I was dreaming but also very much believed the dream to be true. I remember being filled with rage and I imagined—as an observer both outside and inside the dream—harming Steven, cudgeling him with my tennis racket over and over. It was jealousy that sparked this rage, and it was a jealousy I simply did not feel toward him in my waking life. When I did finally wake, I was shaken. What was my unconscious mind telling me? Why had it filled me with the phantom emotions of the old morality I thought I had transcended, the specters of possessiveness and envy and distrust? I told Cam about it later that morning.

"Maybe you're not comfortable with me seeing him after all," he said. "Maybe you just weren't aware of it."

"No, I think it's great that you see him."

"But does it make you jealous?"

"I even like him personally as you know. He's a good guy."

"But jealousy?"

I thought a moment, really surveying my feelings, and answered what felt true. I told him I felt no jealousy. It hadn't always been that way of course. Early in the opening of our relationship I struggled. How could I not? To do so was part of my default factory settings that programmed me to believe monogamy was the only way. I recall once breaking my bathroom mirror when I thought Cam might be seeing someone behind my back, that it was only a matter of time before he left me for someone else. It took time to unlearn what the culture had taught me to expect and presume about masculinity, to second guess my emotional instincts. It took trust and open communication with someone I loved.

"That's what was so strange about the dream," I continued. "Here I was so consumed with rage that I didn't think twice about striking Steven repeatedly with my racket."

Suddenly Cam began to laugh.

"What's so funny?"

"That image. You hitting Steven with your tennis racket."

"Yeah, why the tennis racket? Why not something else? Why not my fist?"

"Why not this?" said Cam, holding up an eggplant, and we both laughed. We were in the kitchen and he was removing carrots and radishes and vegetables I didn't know the name of that had arrived in our weekly CSA delivery. I asked what he thought it all meant. "I don't know," he said in his normal speaking voice, then switched to a faux-Austrian accent: "Sometimes a tennis racket is just a tennis racket."

*

A few mornings later, Cam and I went to a protest in the Financial District outside the building of a banking institution that was underwriting a corporate plan to expand oil drilling on land that had been previously protected. Perhaps prompted by his ongoing nightly discussions with Nancy, in which the personal was inextricably bound up in the political, he'd been channeling a lot of his non-work energy into political action. This wasn't unusual, I should say. Cam had grown up in New York City, in a radical collective, in an entire culture that was attuned to spotlighting wrong and trying to do something about it.

On the other hand, I'd had little interest in politics most of my young adulthood, except to stand generally in tepid opposition to what my parents and those around me in Mississippi had believed. It wasn't until I met Cam that I began to see someone like Che Guevara as anything more than a handsome beret model. In many ways, starting a relationship with him meant undertaking another kind of education, different from the one I had begun in university, where I learned both the technique and history of artistic forms. Cam loaned me books, involved me in long debates over dinner, and challenged me to take part in protest and direct action. "To do nothing is to be complicit!" I remember him admonishing after I expressed reservations about participating in a die-in against the wars. I started to see where I'd come from in a new light. The poverty and racism of Mississippi were not unrelated results of undereducated individuals making poor decisions, as I'd always been encouraged to believe, by well-educated liberals and conservatives alike, but deeply entwined so as to buttress a larger systemic oppression that kept the population divided and powerless and wealth in the right people's hands. I'm trying to imagine what my father would say if he heard me pontificate such a view. He'd probably tell me I was as confused as a fart in a fan factory, so full of shit my eyes were brown.

We'd never believe in the revolutionary violence that Jerry and Nancy had committed themselves to, but we go to protests and knock on doors. We write a lot of checks for causes. Cam volunteers regularly at a homeless shelter and I tutor now and again at 826 Valencia. We are aware of our privilege and how little is at risk for us materially no matter who is in the White House, despite the glaring inequality around us. It used to shame us, our privilege, and still does, I suppose, but we came to make peace with the fact that shame is a powerful motivator for action.

And so there we stood in the cold damp air, holding signs and shouting slogans as people inside the bank occasionally looked down at us for a few moments, cup of coffee in hand, before returning to sending billions in capital back and forth through the ether. Afterward, members of a local socialist group were handing out fliers for an upcoming march against the recent cut in funding for public health clinics, and one of them was our friend Scotty. We cried their name and waved, and they came running over to give us each a hug. We hadn't seen Scotty in a while, so we invited them back to our neighborhood to catch up, and by the time we'd bused back to Bernal Heights the fog had burned off and the weather was warmer. We decided to have a drink out back in the beer garden of Wild Side West. When we arrived, the bar was packed with women—a couple of softball teams from the local league had just arrived for post-game carousing—and I told Cam and Scotty to find a table, that I'd bring our drinks out. "Pear cider for me," said Scotty and they kissed me on the cheek before following Cam out back.

When I first met them, before they'd transitioned, Scotty was a thick man with short dark hair, whom I'd connected with on Grindr. After seeing each other for a while, Cam asked to meet him and the two hit it off. Cam found him handsome and funny, and he asked if he could join us in bed some time. Scotty was excited by the prospects and reluctantly I agreed, the three of us becoming friends and lovers. After we'd known Scotty for almost a year, he informed us that he would soon begin the process of transitioning. This wasn't uncommon—plenty of friends and acquaintances had over the years—but I'd never had a lover transition, and something changed in me when Scotty did: I didn't want to sleep with him anymore. It wasn't a matter of attractiveness because Scotty was a very pretty woman. She'd grown her hair out, had lightened it. She'd lost weight and even seemed, impossibly, taller somehow. Scotty looked terrific, but for some reason it didn't spur the desire it had previously. She was a new person now, but there were vestiges of the one I'd known before. I could hear it in certain moments when her voice would lower unexpectedly or see it in the square jawline of her face in profile, these traces of her former self, and I missed that person. I chastised myself for feeling such a thing, for feeling anything but care and support for my friend as they went on the beautiful but difficult journey of becoming their true self. This was about something way more important than sex and desire, and I resolved to try to be a better friend. Not long ago, when Scotty started identifying as nonbinary, it was as if they had evolved from man to woman and now to something new and magnificent that was beyond gender. Their transcendence and understanding of self were inspiring.

Now at the bar, after placing our drink orders, I took out my phone and checked email. There was a note from the director of the museum. I opened it, feeling nervous, and was relieved that she and the board of trustees had given the OK for me to make an offer on six of Matthew's pieces. Finally, we could start moving forward. I was excited to give him the good news.

When the drinks were ready, I paid and carried the three pints, positioned like a triangle in my hands, out back. There was a group of middle-aged hippies sitting on benches who were passing around a guitar and singing old folk songs. I spied Cam and Scotty farther back in the garden, away from the musicians, though we could still hear them. I set down our glasses and we toasted and drank. As we conversed, I heard the musicians play the familiar chorus to "This Land is Your Land," singing joyfully and communally. They were playing Woody Guthrie's original version that included lines critical of poverty and private property that he later removed because they were too controversial: "One bright sunny morning in the shadow of the steeple / By the relief office I saw my people / As they stood hungry, I stood there wondering / If God blessed America for me."

I was so focused on the song that I hadn't realized Scotty had asked me a question.

"Wake up, Dixon," said Cam snapping his fingers. "Scotty wants to know if you're seeing anyone. It's been a while, hasn't it? Who was that back in the fall? What was her name?"

"I see Malik."

"But he's in New York most of the time," he said. "When was the last time you saw someone here, even just a casual hook-up?"

I thought a moment. The deceit that had once excited me now moved through me like barbed wire.

"Last fall, I guess. Niko."

"Niko, that's her name," said Cam.

"No luck on the apps?" asked Scotty.

"I've just been busy with work. We've got an exhibition next fall that I've been working on for some time."

At the mention of work, Cam pulled out his phone. "Oh my god, I almost forgot," he said. "I've *got* to show you this video we flagged yesterday. You won't believe it. You've never seen anything like it."

*

One day when I was in a meeting with the executive committee and curatorial staff a text bubble appeared on my screen. I was in the middle of listening to the publicity team's ideas for promoting an upcoming Kara Walker retrospective, but I quickly checked to see if it was important.

Checked out La Toya Ruby Frazier, said the text. *You're right. She's amazing. Thanks for the rec.*

It was from Niko. Clearly it could wait, but I was confused, so I picked up my phone and tried to tactfully type with it in my lap, below the conference table. I responded: *I don't remember recommending Frazier. But I agree that she's incredible.* I looked up, back at the Chief of Marketing, who was speaking, and I nodded, though I had no idea what he'd just said, and waited to the feel the buzz of the phone, indicating a response, but there was nothing. I stole a quick look down and there were the co-presence bubbles indicating she was typing, but no text appeared for a long time. Finally, it must have been a minute or two, I felt the buzz in my lap and looked: *Sorry, that was meant for someone else. My mistake. Looking forward to seeing you Thursday!* Quickly I started texting, telling her no problem. I was in the middle of typing *I miss you* when I heard my name. I looked up. It was the head of the executive committee, the museum's director. She was looking at me.

"Pardon?" I said.

"I asked for your thoughts on the report we just listened to."

*

One evening shortly after we'd started seeing each other, Niko and I were in bed at Hotel Boheme and we were having one of those pleasant post-coital conversations, happy and sated, a good kind of exhaustion. She had surprised me with a bottle of sljivovica, the Serbian national drink. Her father distilled his own at home and she always smuggled some back after visits. It's a brandy, redolent of damson plum. Delicious. As Niko spoke, I rose from bed to fix us each a drink in the small water glasses by the sink. She was telling me a story about how when she was seven, without quite understanding why, she'd stolen a single pair of white briefs from a friend's father's dresser. She'd been looking for the bathroom when she accidentally walked into the bedroom. The room was empty, and she began looking around. She picked up some jewelry and trinkets on the dresser and set them back down. She opened her friend's mother's dresser and closed it. Then she opened the top drawer of the husband's side and saw a neat stack of briefs, perhaps ten pairs. She took one and put it in her pocket and then went back to find her friend.

"What did you do with them, the underwear?" I asked.

"I hid them in my closet when I got home, but sometimes at night I would put them on."

"Did you touch yourself?"

"No. It wasn't like that. I hadn't discovered masturbation quite yet. But I knew what attraction was. I had a crush on my friend's father that had less to do with physical desire than an attraction of a different sort. He was kind and funny, unlike my father who was so stern and withdrawn."

"Your father the communist," I said, smiling.

"My father the humorless communist."

"So, you'd wear his underwear and do what?"

"I'd wear his underwear and imagine I was him, walking around my room late at night. I'd talk to myself—addressing me as if I were him—telling me all the fun things we'd do together without his daughter, my friend. I wanted the attention he gave her, that my father didn't give me. But I knew there was something secret and personal about his briefs, that it was wrong that I'd taken them but glad I had. I felt shame for what I'd done but also excitement. I knew my parents would be horrified, would never understand."

"That's the thing about the erotic."

"How so?"

"What makes those moments so intense is that they are doubly charged. Nothing is supremely arousing that isn't also, with the wrong person, supremely disturbing. The power of these experiences is that they sit at the fulcrum where our shame could be utmost and yet we find only assent and approval."

"What was your most erotic moment?" she asked. "Do you remember?"

I thought a moment and then I told her this story:

Back in the early days of our relationship, Cam and I used to host what we called "performance parties." These were gatherings of our friends and acquaintances, preferably from different regions of our lives—that is, people Cam and I knew in some capacity but who didn't necessarily know each other yet. The one requirement for attending the party was that at some point in the evening each person had to perform for the group. Someone might sing a song or recite a favorite poem from memory. Someone else might tap dance or deliver a funny impression. Others revealed their unique hidden talents before strangers: solving a Rubik's cube in a matter of minutes or declaiming chronologically every US president. It could be anything really. Something as simple as a joke even.

These parties were fun, and the aspect of performance served as an icebreaker, disrupting the sectarianism of the familiar that often happens at mixed gatherings of that sort, whereby people talk to the folks they know and politely ignore the rest. But when you've just applauded wildly after watching someone call forth the karate lessons of their youth to break a cinder block in front of a bunch of strangers, you're more inclined to talk to them. The performance parties quickened the normal pace of friendship-courtship and guests often left at the end of the night with a handful of new folks they'd already made plans to see again.

I remember cleaning up after one such party. God, our tiny apartment in the Mission. We'd filled it so full that it resembled the party scene in *Breakfast at Tiffany's*, but I liked it that way. It was late, past one in the morning, and the only guest remaining was a colleague of Cam's from YouTube named Tomas. I didn't know him well, but he seemed nice enough. We were drunk, but Cam and I were lazily washing dishes and collecting trash while Tomas watched us from the sofa, post-gaming the party.

I was hoping he'd leave soon, but he seemed to be in no rush. He begged us to stop cleaning and come hang out, bribing us with molly, and we put down our brooms and sponges and joined him on the couch. Soon we all felt liquidy and amorous. I kissed Cam and afterward he turned to Tomas and said he had nice lips. It was true, but not just his lips. He was very handsome, empirically so. When I said so, Tomas laughed and said that there were no ugly Peruvian men. Again Cam said he had nice lips. This was before we'd opened our relationship and they both looked at each other, but neither moved nor said anything until I said they should kiss. I'd heard Cam talk about Tomas and always suspected he might have a little crush on him, though it didn't bother me, or at least it wasn't bothering me in that moment, and they did kiss, tentatively at first and then more intensely. I watched them, unsure what I was feeling. I would have liked to believe that it was nice to see two beautiful people being affectionate with one another, but then I felt it, the jealousy piercing my middle. They were getting more intense, hands searching over each other's bodies, and I told them to stop. I got up from the couch.

"What?" said Tomas. "You said—"

"I know I did. I just…"

"Come here," said Cam, holding out his arms to me, so I did, and he pulled me toward him. We began to kiss and soon I felt Tomas's lips on my neck. I pulled away, looking at him. A moment of silence. And then the three of us began to laugh hysterically.

"Now you two kiss," said Cam when we'd come out of our laughing fit. "I want to see your lips touch."

I froze but nodded consent, letting Tomas bring his lips to my mouth. I was surprised to find how good, how natural, it felt, this stranger's lips on mine. I was pleased that it pleased me and that I felt no alarm to kiss someone other than my boyfriend. Then all three of us began to kiss and before long we got naked, went to the bedroom, and fooled around before passing out in a sloppy dog-pile of limbs and excess, exhausted by our carnal investigations.

Early the next morning, I woke to find Tomas on top of Cam. I felt a sting of betrayal and anger. Had they waited for me to fall asleep so they could be together, just the two of them? And yet, I was also turned on, watching. I began to touch myself. When I was hard, I moved behind Tomas, embracing his back and kissing his neck as he continued to make love to Cam. "Do it," he said. I feigned ignorance—"What?"—though I knew what he was saying. When I started to move away, he said it again, so I took some lubricant from the bottle that was on the bed and rubbed it over myself. "Do it," he commanded, and when I entered him, I felt my heart evacuate my chest, as if it had been dropped from a very high rooftop. And there we were, each of us connected by our sex. I felt like I was having intercourse with both of them. We had a flow, a synchronicity of movement. We were like Ivy League champion rowers.

Tomas left later that morning and it was just Cam and me, alone. He was sitting at the kitchen table with a cup of coffee warming his hand. I poured myself one and joined him. We both smiled a little sheepishly and then I said, "So that was weird. I didn't know that's where the night would end up."

In some sense it had felt like an extension of the party: we were playing new roles, trying on different identities, performing.

"Yeah, but I kind of liked it," he said. "Did you?"

"I don't know."

Many of my friends were open, but I'd come from such a conservative place that monogamy was hardwired into our DNA. It wasn't until we were in the act with Tomas, inhibitions compromised, that I could see it any other way. Perhaps that's all it took. A door I thought forever shut had been opened and we decided we'd walk through it and embrace this awakening. *Say yes* became our mantra. Say yes to any experience you wanted, so long as we were honest about it and it didn't hurt someone else. We wanted a life of passion, a catalogue of intense experiences. We tried sleeping with other people, sometimes separately, sometimes together. We'd both been in previous relationships that had been damaged by cheating and lies, so having an open relationship just made sense; it seemed strange that we'd ever thought otherwise.

"But you will always be my person," said Cam. "You know that, right?" I felt moved by his love and by my love for him, and I nodded, eyes misty, as I moved to embrace him. "I love what's happening to us," Cam said, stroking his hand over my back as I cried tears of love and gratitude into his chest. "We're turning into something new. This is it."

"What is it?"

"Our becoming."

I told Niko this story that day last fall and then largely forgot about the conversation until one afternoon this spring when, donning VR glasses in a backroom at Encounter, I wandered into Niko's recreation of the experience. I didn't know ahead of time; she wanted it to be a surprise and certainly it was. When I realized what she'd done, what she'd created, I was touched, but I wasn't the least bit turned on. I'd never tried VR and I found the experience strange and discombobulating. The simulacra of Tomas and Cam looked nothing like the flesh-and-blood people I'd been with, which was understandable since she'd never seen them before. But even my virtual body in the scenario, a body she knew so well, looked different from my own. My abdominals were sharply defined, as if I did nothing but crunches all day, and my penis was bigger and thicker than it actually is. It had the opposite effect of her intentions. I found myself wondering if this was the body Niko wished me to have all those times we made love. Was I, a few years into my fifties, disappointing to her? I couldn't watch anymore. I took off the headset and goggles and sat in a chair scrolling on my phone until my thirty-minute allotment of virtual eroticism was finished.

Afterward, I was to meet Niko for lunch. I'd proposed this to thank her for the gift, and as I walked up the block to Delfina I tried to put on a good face. I told myself to remember how kind the gesture was and how much time she must have spent putting together a scenario that she created for me alone. Niko was sitting at an outside table on the sidewalk when I saw her and waved, smiling. She only raised her eyebrows in response. I could sense something was off from the first, and I overcompensated by being extra effusive about my experience at Encounter. I went on and on about how wonderful it was until I sensed she knew I was propitiating. I felt foolish lying, so I told her the truth, that I hadn't even been able to make it through the entire scenario.

"I'm sorry," I said. "But I told you, I have trouble getting aroused by screens and images. Plus, it was my first time trying VR. I didn't know what the hell I was doing."

"It's okay," she said with some distance. I'd offended her, I could see.

"Hey," I said, reaching across the table to take her hand. "All I want is to be here in the present with you, not some recreation of the past. You know me. All I want is the real."

"I'll tell you something real, Dixon," she said. "My sister's dead."

*

Cam and I were getting ready to enter the Twenty-fourth Street BART station when his phone began to buzz. Quickly he looked at it. "It's Rebecca, I gotta take it." Another in the seemingly endless string of school shootings had just happened and we were on our way to a march in support of gun control measures being debated in Congress. "Hello," Cam said into the phone. It was loud, and he had to press a finger to his ear as hipsters, homeless, and tech workers streamed past us in every direction, hither and thither. I watched a woman rise from the ground—she'd been holding a sign that said *Spare a down payment on a burrito?*—and drop the waist of her burgundy sweatpants, defecating right on the sidewalk without anyone, other than I apparently, seeming to notice. There was a sudden change in the light, and I looked to the sky where I saw a drone diminish in the distance. In a matter of seconds Cam was off the phone.

"Everything okay?" I asked.

"Nancy's dead."

"I'm so sorry, Cam," I said, moving to embrace him, but he was already walking away from me toward the station.

"Come on," he said. "We're going to be late. The march starts in ten."

*

While Niko flew to Serbia to bury her sister, Cam and I travelled to New York to cremate his mother. Nancy's funeral was a crowded affair. Gone were members of the old Communist left, those of her parents' generation who had long since passed, but there were plenty New Left radicals of her own, as well as us, their children and grandchildren, progressives and leftists, as well as the occasional black sheep anarcho-capitalist/libertarian, each generation both sympathetic to and skeptical of the politics of the one that preceded. Many people came to pay their respect, even those who'd fallen out with Nancy decades ago. Cam had only recently started to communicate with his father again, agreeing to visit him after the funeral. Jerry had asked Cam to keep tabs on who attended, and when we saw him at the prison the following day he scanned through the list, muttering after each name he read. "Asshole." "Sonofabitch." "Fascist." "Saint." And so on. Everyone received his judgment.

"I'm still angry with you," Cam said.

"I can't do anything about that. Your anger is your problem."

"You're not hearing me, Pop."

"Oh, I hear you. You want to be mad at me, fine. I've received harsher judgement. *Breitbart* says I should be taken out and shot on the steps of the Capitol. Your anger I can take, believe me."

"Can you take me not visiting you? Can you take me not answering your calls again?"

Jerry looked at the floor and said nothing. The visitation room was reminiscent both in appointment and spirit of a high school cafeteria. We had our own table, the three of us, but the large room was a cacophonous din of laughter, crying, and complaint—reunions of every sort.

"Why didn't you tell me Nancy was my mother?" said Cam. "Why did I have to wait till she was on her deathbed to know the truth?"

"That was Nancy's choice, not mine."

"You could have told me. You could have told me years ago when I would have had time to know her, but you didn't."

"I made a promise and that means something," he said. "I don't break vows to a comrade." He said this with such conviction that I couldn't imagine it was possibly untrue. "Besides, she wasn't your mother. She gave birth to you. And you should be happy to have her blood in your veins. She was brilliant and brave. Not like"—he waved the list of names—"these…these craven rats!"

And then, suddenly, he began to sob, saying Nancy's name over and over again, wiping his face with the list so that the black ink smeared his cheek. I didn't know what to do. It seemed to come from nowhere, this outburst of tearful emotion that I couldn't have ever imagined witnessing from such a hardened man. Jerry had always struck me as incredibly intelligent and attune to the suffering of people in the abstract, brilliant in many ways, but he was stunningly blind and unintelligent when it came to the feelings of flesh-and-blood human beings standing right before him. He was the least sentimental man I'd ever met, and yet here he was crying before us for his lost friend and ally, the mother of his son. I don't know if Cam had ever seen him this way either. He made no move to comfort him. We were too stunned to do anything but watch. Jerry was embarrassed and wanted us to leave. "Go away," he said, between sobs. "Go away but come back tomorrow. You will, won't you?"

"No, Pop. I'm not coming back tomorrow."

"Please. You must."

"I have to get back home. I have work."

He averted his face from us as he continued to cry and stammer. "She's gone. It's just me now. It's just me. Guard!"

*

On the morning I was to pick up Niko at the airport, I played my usual Wednesday tennis match with Tim Tyree. It was one of those cloudy days that nonetheless left me sunburned. I lost, which always puts me in a bad mood. I was still a little perturbed by it when I arrived at SFO to find Niko waiting at the curb with a garment bag and rollaboard in hand, and I began recounting in detail for her my defeat at the hands of Tim that morning.

"Dixon, I'm sorry," she interrupted as I navigated us to the freeway, "but I wouldn't normally give a fuck about tennis, and I especially don't right now." She looked at me and then back out the window. I let it be quiet for some time before remarking that in all our time together I hadn't known she'd had a sister. She'd never mentioned it.

"Tell me about her," I said.

"Bisa was her name," said Niko. "Short for Biserka."

"Biserka? What a name. Did she have a temper like your father?"

"No, not a temper. She had something else, something different. In Serbia we have a word for this: inat. It is like defiance. A stubborn, sometimes spiteful, defiance. That's what she had."

"May I ask how she died?"

"She was a certain kind of suicide," she said.

A certain kind of suicide? I wondered but thankfully didn't have to ask for elaboration because Niko began to tell me her sister's story. Biserka, she said proudly, had once been the best seamstress in Belgrade. So good, in fact, that Lamborghini had brought her to Italy to sew the interiors of their cars. Their quality control aimed for nothing short of perfection. Not a stich could be off or the whole thing had to be scrapped and begun anew. For years Biserka never made a mistake until one day she did. She was given the benefit of the doubt, but then it happened again not long after. Her skills were deteriorating but she wasn't old; she was thirty-four, what should have been the prime of her life and career. She didn't understand what was wrong, so she went to see a doctor, who after some tests diagnosed her with early onset Alzheimer's. It was something that ran in their family. Their grandfather had had it, as had an uncle.

"It could have happened to either or us," Niko said, "but she got it and I didn't."

I remained silent, hoping she would continue, and after a short pause she did.

"Bisa had seen the disease firsthand, knew what awaited her. She'd taken up religion when she moved to Italy, mostly to fit in socially, but now with her fate fixed she became obsessed. She left her job at Lamborghini to become a missionary and chose to do her work in unsafe, war-torn countries, the most dangerous places she could get access to. She once told me that if she weren't religious, she'd have killed herself when she got the diagnosis, but as a person of faith she couldn't. Instead, she put herself in risky positions where she could very well die in service of her religion. And eventually she did. It was a death wish, which, I suppose, for someone as religious as her, is really an eternal life wish."

"Where was she? What happened?"

"Afghanistan. She was crushed from falling rubble after a hospital was bombed. She'd been trying to help evacuate patients. They recovered her body and returned it to Serbia for burial. My father is an atheist, but he was decent enough to let her have the church funeral she desired. The night after we put her in the ground, I went out to the splaves in Belgrade. You've heard of these?"

"Yes, they're quite famous. Discotheques on barges in the water, right?"

"I went to the splaves and danced all night. It was something we'd done as kids, long before Bisa found religion, and that was the version of her I'd known and loved. Not the suicidal martyr. So I went out in my black mourning dress and danced until my shoes broke and then I danced barefoot until my feet ached. Afterward, I limped through the streets of Belgrade, past the old citadel until I got to the confluence of the Sava and Danube and could walk no further. I slept on a bench and woke sometime later, my feet raw and bloody, my arms bug-bitten."

I didn't know what to say. It was as though she were narrating the memory to herself and I wasn't present. I took out my phone to check the time. It was only after I put it back in my pocket that I realized I'd looked at the numbers but not registered their meaning. I still wasn't sure what time it was. Niko slumped against the car window, staring out at the rain, no doubt thinking about what had happened, the long journey home to bury her sister. I wanted to make her feel good. I recalled our trip to Malik's cabin in the Russian River Valley and how pleasant it had been to get away. Perhaps we were due to get out of the city again. Maybe this time we could go somewhere else, leave California even.

"That sounds nice," she said, moving to rest her cheek on my chest as I drove with one hand.

"We could go to Chicago or New York. Anywhere. Hell, we could go to Birmingham if we wanted. There are some pieces at the museum there I'm wanting to look at and inquire about borrowing for the southern photography exhibition next fall."

"Birmingham," said Niko. "That's in Alabama, yes?"

"Correct."

"Where Matthew was born."

"We could go see where he's from, Hale County, the area he photographs."

A few weeks prior, perhaps a month even, I'd received approval to make the offer to purchase six of Matthew's pieces, and we were moving forward. The museum was happy to acquire the work of a promising new artist. Valerie was thrilled to sell his work at all but especially to a museum instead of a collector who might flip it on the secondary market for more money once Matthew's profile rose from being included in the show. Matthew was relieved not to be dropped from his gallery and get his fifty percent cut of the sale. It was a victory for all parties involved. I told this to Niko and when I was finished, she responded by saying, "I know." I hadn't spoken to her about Matthew since we'd had drinks, the three of us, at Tosca some weeks ago. I wondered how she'd found out. Then I realized what I knew but didn't know.

"It was him," I said. "That text you mistakenly sent me, the one about liking LaToya Ruby Frazier. That was meant for Matthew."

"Yes."

"You all are in touch? Since when?"

"Since we had drinks with him. He emailed me after I got back, and we exchanged numbers."

"How did he get your email address?"

"How did you?" I recalled that day last fall when the snooty young man at Encounter pulled up her contact information in a matter of seconds. *You're welcome, sir.* "He asked if we were together," she said.

"And how did you respond?"

"I said you were in an open marriage, and I can see whomever I want."

"You talked about me, my personal life?"

"How could we not?"

"I'm not just some guy who likes his work. We've entered a business relationship. I don't get personal when that's the case."

"Well, it's done."

A few beats of silence followed before I couldn't help opening my mouth again.

"Are you seeing him?"

"What does that even mean? I see him some."

"Why didn't you tell me?"

"It never came up. I didn't think it was a big deal. Besides, you said I could see other people."

"This is different."

"Not the way I see it."

A few beats passed, my mind spinning, before I could speak.

"I mean, are you fucking him?"

"Dixon—"

"Are you?"

"Ask yourself if you really want to know the answer to that question."

If I'd been standing up, I might have fallen backward.

"You are. Jesus. Why wouldn't you just say so?"

"I don't think I should have to report every person I sleep with to you."

"There are others?"

She exhaled heavily.

"I'm tired. I really don't want to talk about this right now."

When we got to her place in Japantown, I asked if I could come in. Despite the way our conversation went astray, I wanted to take care of her after her difficult trip home, but she said she was fine, that she just needed to rest for a day or two. She'd be in touch. I watched through the entryway window as she buzzed into her apartment building and ascended a flight of stairs until I saw only her legs and then her shoes and then she was out of sight.

*

I keep a pen and notepad on my bedside table in the event an idea comes to me during the night or in the morning, as they often do. Sometimes the notes are quotidian or practical—a reminder to pick up dry cleaning or some such errand—and other times they are more significant and meaningful: notes on an artist's work for an exhibition catalogue, ideas for future shows and the like. They often arrive when I'm in various states of drowsiness. Sometimes I'm asleep and they come to me via dream, an idea for my waking life smuggled into the fantasia of my unconscious. And when that happens, I must decide whether to wake up and write down the idea, risking being unable to fall back to sleep, or to stay asleep and risk losing the idea.

One morning when I was having a dream about Malik, in which he was painting a portrait of Jerry in his cell, something came to me and I decided to wake myself and explore it. I switched on my bedside light, grabbed the notepad and pen, and wrote down *Many Souths*. That was the title I was thinking of calling the exhibition on cross-generational southern photography. I started listing the names and works of artists I wished to include in the show, starting with the older, well-established photographers and working up to the newer artists. At the bottom I wrote *Matthew Smith* and stared at it. In my mind's eye I saw his pictures I'd purchased on behalf of the museum. I'd chosen excellently; my eye had not let me down. Then I thought of the one I purchased for myself that was now hanging in the living room but had trouble imagining it. That is, I knew the subject and content of the picture, but I couldn't see it in the moment because I kept thinking about Matthew in bed with Niko, the two of them talking about me afterward. What were they saying? Cam stirred in bed next to me. I caressed his back. The light was coming up, the city covered in a burial shroud of fog, so I got up, put on my clothes and shoes, and went for a walk around the neighborhood to clear my head.

A few nights later, Cam and I went to a Passover Seder hosted by a married couple named Janet and Barbara. They'd been involved in the movement with Jerry and Nancy, more of Cam's many "aunts" from the collective who were now part of a radical diaspora. Janet and Barbara lived in a renovated Victorian in the Western Addition, and we were greeted at the door with warm hugs from them and sloppy licks from their twin terriers Bolshie and Zetkin. For years they'd invited us to their pro-Palestinian Seders, along with a dozen or so other friends, and it was always a meaningful evening of food and conversation, somber remembrance and prayer. We set out the saltwater, as well as Elijah's wine glass and Miriam's cup. We added Palestinian olive oil to the usual Seder plate. We talked a lot about Nancy. Everyone—not just the men—donned yarmulkes and said prayers for her and for others who were still inside. We prayed for the oppressed and suffering of the world. We read from *Exodus*, and cried listening to poems by Samih al-Qasim and Mahmoud Darwish. When it was finished, we embraced one another, tears in our eyes.

Afterward, we had coffee and drinks. Someone got out a board game and others conversed. Cam and I were sitting on the couch talking to Janet when my phone buzzed. I'd taken it out of my pocket when we sat down, but I hadn't flipped it over. When the screen illuminated with an incoming message, we all looked at it instinctively.

"Niko," said Cam, seeing the sender's name. "You all are still in touch?"

I picked up my phone. *We need to talk*, read her message. *ASAP.*

"I haven't heard from her in months."

"What's she want?"

"I'm not sure," I said, putting my phone in my pocket as I turned to Janet. "Sorry, that was rude of me. What were you saying?"

I pretended to listen, nodding and uh-huhing occasionally, until enough time had passed for me to excuse myself. I went to the bathroom, where I sat on the toilet lid and responded to Niko's text, setting up a time to meet the following day. When I resumed my position on the couch next to Cam, I rubbed my hand over his back, and he smiled at me.

Janet was staring at me, a little grin on her face. Bolshie or Zetkin—I can never tell them apart—was sitting in her lap.

"For a WASP, Dixon, you make an okay Jew."

I wasn't sure how to respond, but then it came.

"L'chaim," I said, raising my glass of wine.

*

Niko had asked to meet in the Ferry Building at the Blue Bottle coffee stand, the same location we'd met at on our first date, and she was waiting with a coffee in hand when I arrived the following afternoon.

"Why?" she said. "Why did you do it?"

She wouldn't hug me, pulling away when I tried to embrace her. She was agitated and angry, practically shaking.

"Tell me," she said. "I want to know."

"Calm down."

I placed a hand on her arm, but she shook it off.

"Talk to me or I'm leaving, and you'll never see me again."

"I'll talk," I said. "But not here. Not in this crowd."

I suggested we take the ferry to Sausalito, in part because I thought it would be a better, quieter place to talk and in part because it would confine us to the same space, so she couldn't storm off. Reluctantly, she agreed. She was wearing her usual outfit, dark denim and a black button-down rolled to the elbows, but she donned a hat I'd never seen before. It was military green, like something Fidel might have worn. It was chilly on deck—the Bay's finicky microclimates and bone-chilling air coming off the Pacific—and I offered her my jacket as we sat down.

"Take it," I said. "Haven't you learned that you need to layer in San Francisco?"

She wouldn't accept it, just crossed her arms at her chest.

"I want to know," she said.

"What do you want to know?"

"You know why I'm upset. You canceled the museum's purchase of Matthew's work. Why?"

"I didn't cancel it. He and Valerie will get their money. We signed contracts. What I did was deaccession the work."

"What does that even mean?"

I gave a truncated explanation of the process by which a museum removes a work of art from its collection.

"What happens to them now, the photographs?"

"They will be sold or otherwise disposed of."

"Otherwise disposed of?" The anger had drained out of her momentarily, replaced by shock and confusion. "I suppose this means you're kicking him out of the exhibition as well." It seemed a statement not requiring an answer because the answer was obvious. I sat there silently. "Why would you do that? You just purchased the photographs and now you're getting rid of them?"

"I had second thoughts."

"Bullshit."

"The board had reservations that I dismissed initially."

"What reservations?"

"I'm not at liberty to discuss. Like I said, there were second thoughts."

"The only thoughts you had were of me and Matthew together. He needed this, Dixon."

"He'll get his money. We signed a contract."

"Not just the money. He needed his art to be in a museum. For the exposure. For his gallery. For his career."

"There are plenty of museums."

"Fuck you," she said and hit me in the chest with the side of her hand. "You know what being in the permanent collection at SFMOMA does for an artist."

"He'll be fine. I'm not worried."

"And you did this not because of the board of trustees or the museum director or who-the-fuck-ever. You told me I could see whomever I wanted."

"Yes, but not him."

"Why?"

"Because we have a business relationship. I told you." After a beat I added: "Had a business relationship."

"I don't believe you."

"It's the truth."

"What do you know about truth?" She took her hat off, setting it on her lap for a moment, and then put it back on. "Why do this to Matthew? It makes no sense."

"I told you. Second thoughts. Purely a business decision about what's best for the museum."

"I don't believe you. It was a decision of the heart and your heart is cruel. Why?"

I said nothing.

"Because he's a great artist, the kind you never became?"

"You're trying to hurt me."

"Because he's younger than you?"

"Get it out of your system."

"Because you want to be the one fucking him?"

I laughed.

"That's it, isn't it? You want Matthew."

"I want—" I began and corrected myself. "I wanted his art. Not him."

"For a man like you there's no difference!"

She shot up from her seat and stalked to the railing. I followed her. Her back was to me, and she stared out at the water. Just then the wind blew her hat from her head, and she didn't even reach for it. I looked at it, floating below us.

"Niko."

"I want off this boat."

"Please."

"I can't be around you. You are vicious. Your heart is a fist."

"Let's start over. Talk to me, please."

"Between this conversation and nothing, I choose nothing."

I offered a weak apology, but she wouldn't engage me any further. When the ferry got to Sausalito, she wouldn't get off. I tried to tell her we could have lunch, that we'd calmed down and were clearheaded again, but she stayed where she was until the ferry set off again, headed back to the Embarcadero. Finally I stopped trying. We stood at the railing, watching the water, saying nothing, and when we got to the pier and docked, she turned quickly and left without another word.

*

I didn't try to contact her for several days afterward. I figured we both needed a little perspective on the situation, the awful things we'd said. She was right; my jealousy had debased me. The same part of me that had wanted to help Matthew had come to desire his professional destruction. I don't know whether it was for one of the reasons Niko alleged or all of them. I'm not sure it matters. What did was the reality of my actions, and while I regretted some of my behavior, I did not regret backing out of the acquisition of Matthew's work. I couldn't possibly have played midwife, birthing his beautiful art into the world on the walls of my museum, as he and Niko fell deeper in love, each of them pulling farther away from me and closer to one another.

A week later, I called and left Niko a message, apologizing and asking if we could meet so I could say it in person. I figured it was a longshot, but to my surprise after three days of silence she texted back and agreed to meet for lunch. We met at L'Ardoise in the Castro. She was terse and icy initially but became more forthcoming over lunch as we talked. I apologized for the things I'd said and done.

"You can keep seeing him," I said. "Matthew."

"I wasn't asking for permission."

"I will do nothing to obstruct."

"You've done enough already."

I told her I couldn't go back on the events I'd already set in motion to deaccession the pieces. Valerie was furious with me, but she couldn't afford to hold a grudge forever. The executive committee and board were not happy either. It was incredibly rare, practically nonexistent, to deaccession work so soon after purchase. I wasn't in danger of losing my job, but I'd made a mistake, looked rash, and was trying to do the things that would get me back in their good graces. I'd mitigated some of the damage by locating a buyer who was interested in acquiring the work, which would allow us to recoup most of the money we'd spent.

Niko and I split a bottle of Pellegrino over lunch, but neither of us ordered wine or cocktails, and despite the lack of alcohol we grew a little tipsy, on memory if nothing else, as the acrimony began to fade, and we reinhabited our affection for one another. We fell back into a warmth and touched one another when we spoke and smiled and laughed, as if Matthew and his photographs had never existed.

"I have an idea," I said after paying the check. I used to love going to matinees back when I lived in New York. There was nothing better than playing hooky and settling into the dark of a theater while the rest of the city worked away. I took her by the hand, and we wandered into the street toward the Castro Theater. She'd never been. I loved the building, its 1930s décor and Wurlitzer organ. The last time I'd come they were showing *Whatever Happened to Baby Jane?* and the theater had been packed with people, half of whom were men in drag, Cam and I included, dressed up in the outfits and garish, psycho-biddy makeup of Bette Davis and Joan Crawford. Today they were showing *Vertigo*. It was halfway finished, but I bought tickets anyway. There were only a few other people in the theater. We took a seat a few rows behind an old man sitting alone, and as we watched Jimmy Stewart scavenge the streets of old San Francisco searching for Kim Novak, I placed my hand on Niko's leg and rubbed. She placed her hand on my thigh and rubbed and then we were kissing. Oblivious to others and drunk on the finality of love, or something like it, we quietly rose and walked up the aisle to the area behind the last row of seats. There was no one there. She lifted up the hem of her skirt, pulled her underwear to the side, and we made love quietly to the frantic sounds of the film's denouement. I didn't care if anybody saw. My heart and body felt full.

The intensity of the experience allowed me to believe for a moment that we could continue as lovers and friends, but afterward, as the spell of the afternoon wore off, we were once again on opposite sides of a divide I had forged. We were standing on the sidewalk outside the theater. "Fuck," said Niko, as if realizing what had just happened was not some VR scenario she'd created for work. "I promised myself I wouldn't do that." We hadn't used a condom and she said she needed to go to a drugstore and get a Plan B pill. "I'm losing at life." I asked when I could see her again. Perhaps at Hotel Boheme? She stopped digging through her bag and looked up at me slowly, an incredulous expression on her face.

"I'm in love with Matthew," she said.

"Love? You're sure? So quick."

"Look, Dixon. Let me be clear. I no longer wish you ill, but I don't want you in my life. I mean it. This is it. It's over between us." Saying this seemed to release a burden she'd been carrying, and she laughed as she walked away from me with a buoyant little step.

"Good luck," she said, one arm flailing above her head. I couldn't tell if it was disingenuous or not. She walked with excitement and purpose now; she looked half crazy, like she was suddenly ready to march on City Hall for some cause she was passionate about. I watched until she turned a corner and was gone. That was almost a month ago. I haven't seen her since.

In the aftermath of all this I started seeing a therapist, and recently she asked me what I'd lost in losing Niko.

"I'm not sure," I said. "Someone I enjoyed being around. A sense of excitement."

"More than that. More than the sex."

"I lost Matthew and his art. That still pains me deeply."

"Yes, but what else did you lose?"

I was quiet, turning it over in my head.

"Your husband doesn't know," she continued. "Niko's not going to say anything. Unlike most affairs, you got away with it. You didn't destroy your happy life. So, what did it cost you?"

"I don't know," I said, then ventured quietly, stupidly, hopefully: "Nothing?"

She studied me in a piercing way, eyes scanning over the contours of my face, looking for some answer there that my mouth was unable or unwilling to relay. She shook her head and pushed the bridge of her glasses back so that her eyes suddenly seemed huge.

"I think we both know that's not true."

*

Yesterday I went to Golden Gate Park by myself. Smoke filled the sky from the wildfires that are raging through Sonoma, Napa, and Mendocino once again. They're so regular now that it's become our fifth season. I'd gone to see an exhibition at the de Young Museum and then strolled through the botanical garden, a place I love to visit but to do so now felt strange, almost apocalyptic. All that beauty seemed destined for imminent ruin. Afterward, I walked to the Inner Sunset to a café and bought an espresso and then continued to walk through the Haight and into Cole Valley before crossing Market and heading back to the Mission. Many people I passed wore surgical masks, and I found the smoke did make breathing more difficult. Nonetheless, I kept on. My legs were beginning to ache, my feet sore, but I liked that they were so. It made me remember I had a body, that I wasn't just trapped in my head all the time. I walked by our old apartment building, past all the cheap restaurants Cam and I had so loved when we first moved to the city and were trying to save money. Some were no longer in business or had been turned into something else, but I remembered the taste of our favorite dishes: the tika masala of Pakwan, the slices of olive and onion pizza at Dejavue, the noodle soup of Sunflower, the veggie burritos of Cancun.

I was walking by Delores Park when a funny thing happened. I saw him, Cam that is. It was as though I'd imagined him into the present by lingering in our past. He was sitting on a blanket with a man, who wasn't Steven. This was a person I'd never seen before. He had a shaved head as well, though his was buzzed, not straight-razored to the scalp, and he had on clear glasses. They both wore white masks that covered their nose and mouth, but I was certain it was my husband. Despite the masks and coiffures, they didn't look sickly or infirm. They looked strong, vital, alive, but also, somehow, inexplicably, not entirely human. They looked like cyborgs sharing a picnic. Periodically one or the other would pick up a piece of bread or cheese and momentarily lift the mask to slip it into their mouth. There was a clear warmth between the two that could have been attraction, though they neither kissed nor touched one another in the time I was there. Cam hadn't mentioned anything about a date. I watched a little longer, unsure whether to make my presence known, before continuing on. The scent of scorched earth was everywhere; I'd smell it in my clothes and taste it when I bit into an apple after I got home.

Later that night, we were washing dishes after dinner: me dunking plates and glasses into the soapy basin, Cam drying and putting them in the cupboard.

"Your birthday's coming up next month," said Cam. "What do you want to do?"

"Let's go to a bar and drink fifty-three shots of tequila."

"Seriously, Dixon. We need to celebrate. We should go somewhere or do something."

"I don't know."

"What if we hosted a performance party. Like the old days."

"We haven't done that in ages."

"It would be so much fun."

"Perhaps."

"We could invite all our friends. Malik could fly out."

"Poor Malik."

"What's wrong?"

"He called today. Bad news."

"What is it?"

"The cabin in Russian River."

"No," he said.

"The fire went right through his valley."

Cam made a whimpering sound.

"He won't be able to see for himself until the fires stop, but he knows it's gone."

"Then he should stay with us. As long as he needs. We can help him re—"

"Yes," I said, putting more soap on the sponge, "I'll let him know." I washed quietly for a few moments and then told Cam that I'd seen him in the park.

"What?"

"Dolores Park. I saw you there."

"When?"

"Today. You were having a picnic with a man. A handsome man."

I continued to wash, but Cam stopped, a turquoise plate in one hand and the white towel in the other.

"You looked like you were enjoying yourself," I said. "You looked like you were on a date."

"I wasn't in the park today."

"It's okay. I'm not upset about it."

"No, you're not listening," he said. "I wasn't in the park. I was in San Bruno all day. At the office. I ate at my desk."

"That's strange."

"It's not strange actually. That's how I take most lunches. Besides, if I'd gone on a date, I would have told you."

"I could have sworn I saw you."

I thought of the two men with their shiny heads, their faces partially covered by masks.

"Must have been someone else," he said. "My doppelganger."

"I guess so."

"Hey," he said, putting away the plate and flinging the towel over his shoulder. He placed his arms around me, embracing me, though my hands were under water and I couldn't reciprocate. "Is everything okay? Anything you want to talk about?"

There was a stubborn bit of food stuck to one of the dinner plates and I scrubbed at it furiously with the scouring pad before rinsing it and examining it under the light. Good enough, I thought, and handed him the plate.

"Dixon?"

"I'm fine," I said, and we went back to washing and drying. "Everything's fine."

That night, while Cam watched a show in the bedroom, I found myself standing in our living room looking at the photograph of Matthew's I'd purchased. It was undeniably excellent, but the miasma of everything that had happed, however adventitious to the subject and content of the photograph itself, made it unbearable to look at. I would have to try to sell it on the secondary market or give it away at a loss of ten-thousand dollars. It was worth it not to have to face it each day. Next to it hung a portrait of me Malik had painted early in our friendship. I couldn't have been more than twenty-five. It will be included in his first European retrospective next year. Looking at the painting, I felt my age, the sorrow of youth evanescing. Beside that was a framed article *Artforum* had done on an exhibition of mine five years ago. I found it a little embarrassing to have it hanging on the wall of my house, but Cam had had it framed for me as a surprise anniversary gift and that loving kindness meant more to me than a little embarrassment.

I heard Cam laugh from the bedroom and I wanted to join him, but I couldn't just yet. I found myself transfixed, as I often am, by the last work hanging on the wall, the first piece of art I ever obtained, a gift given to me thirty years ago when I was living in New Orleans, dreaming of becoming a photographer, and in love with a married woman. Pelin. I heard the name in my head and then whispered it aloud into the quiet of the living room. It was William Eggleston's famous photograph, "The Red Ceiling." She'd given it to me at a time when I understood neither its value nor excellence. Today a copy is held at the Museum of Modern Art in New York as well as the Getty in Los Angeles. A third hangs on my wall. Like many others outside the art world, Cam recognized it only as the cover of Big Star's record *Radio City*. There was something both beautiful and menacing about the photo. That unreal shade of red that looks as though it might drip from the print. What is the exact shade? Carmine, cochineal, crimson lake. Red, red, red. Like a ripe Morello cherry, like blood shot from a beating heart. Inevitably it made me think of my younger self. Every time I looked at it I felt like I was brushing shoulders with a life I could have lived but didn't. Again, Cam laughed and this time I pulled myself away from the picture to join him in the bedroom.

The following morning—that is to say this morning—I was awakened when I felt Cam's lips on mine. What a pleasant way to enter consciousness, the world. I kissed him back and soon we were making love in the wonderful languor of daybreak. Afterward, he rolled out of bed and disappeared into the bathroom. The door was cracked; I could see a sliver of light. The land line began to ring. "Sorry, Pop," said Cam. "Now's not a good time." He is only now beginning to find rapprochement with Jerry. I listened to the phone ring and when it stopped all I heard was the soft and lonely sound of Cam's urine hitting the toilet water. Then I heard his voice. He was describing one of the videos he'd had to take down from YouTube the previous day. Someone had uploaded one showing the aftermath of a suicide bombing in an outdoor cafe. Limbs, blood, horror.

"What on earth made you think of that now?" I called out.

"It's not the kind of thing you forget."

I said nothing.

"I thought of it because there are a lot of awful things in the world," he said. "But I love you, and—"

I couldn't hear the rest of what he said because the roar of the toilet flushing swallowed it.

"What?"

He repeated himself, but now I couldn't hear over the din of the faucet as he washed his hands.

"I still didn't catch that last part," I said, raising my voice to a near yell.

The water stopped, and I heard the ruffle of the hand towel. Then the door opened, and I saw his smiling face.

"I said, I love our life."

Acknowledgements

First and foremost, I'd like to thank the people who read parts or entire drafts (sometimes multiple) of this book over the years: Chris Brunt, Kevin Gonzalez, Clarke Levidiotis, Jim Mattson, Hendree Milward, Stuart Nadler, Sigrid Nunez, Hannah Pittard, Ellis Purdie, Robin Rahija, Kathleen Sachs, and Ted Thompson. The book would not exist without your feedback and encouragement.

Thank you to the National Endowment for the Arts for crucial monetary support, as well as the institutions that gave me time, space, and community in which to work on You Are Loved: I-Park Foundation, Norton Island Residency Program, Vermont Studio Center, Newnan ArtRez, Hambidge Center for the Arts, Millay Arts, and the Fairhope Center for the Writing Arts.

Thank you to James Brubaker and everyone at Southeast Missouri State University Press, who worked tirelessly to make sure the best version of this book came into the world. Thank you to Elina Cohen for her wonderful cover design.

And lastly, thank you to my friends and family. You are loved.